KING LEAR

KING LEAR

A play by William Shakespeare

adapted and illustrated by Gareth Hinds

CANDLEWICK PRESS

Dramatis Personae

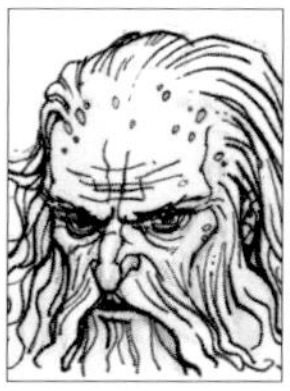

LEAR
King of Britain

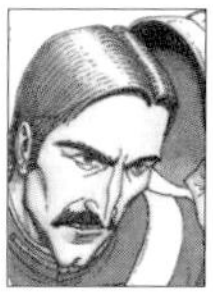

Earl of
KENT

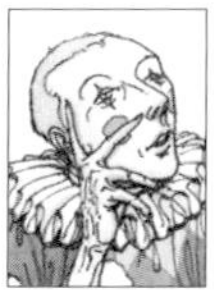

Fool
Lear's jester

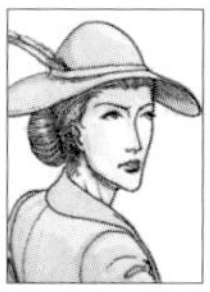

GONERIL
Lear's eldest daughter

=

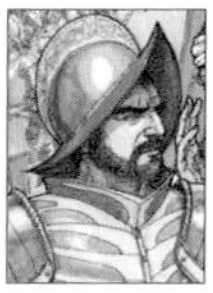

Duke of
ALBANY

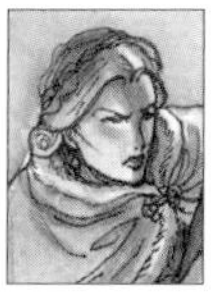

REGAN
Lear's second daughter

=

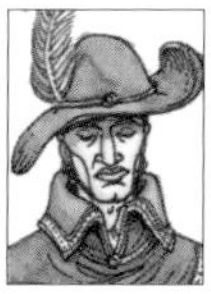

Duke of
CORNWALL

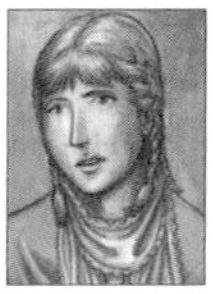

CORDELIA
Lear's youngest daughter

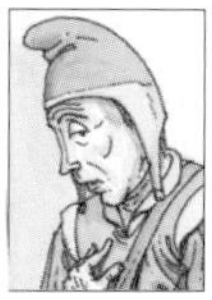

OSWALD
servant to Goneril

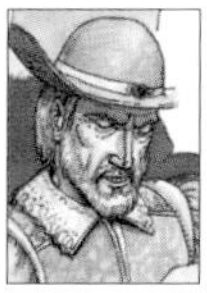

Earl of
GLOUCESTER

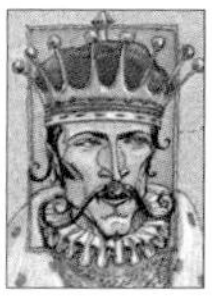

King of
FRANCE
suitor to Cordelia

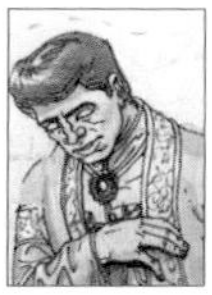

Duke of
BURGUNDY
suitor to Cordelia

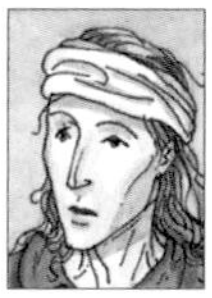

EDGAR
Gloucester's son

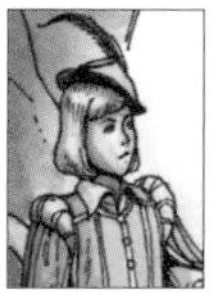

EDMUND
Gloucester's illegitimate son

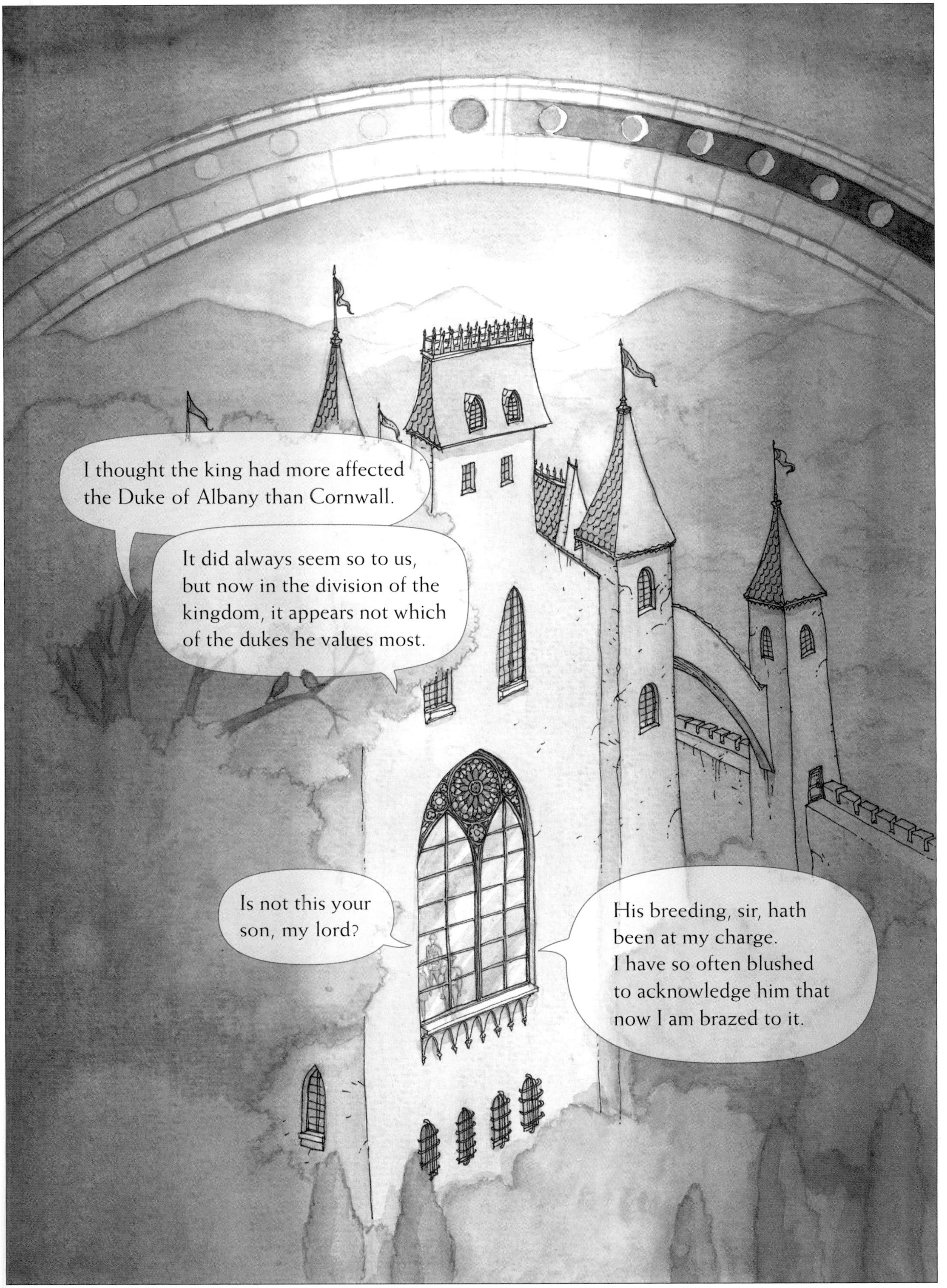
I thought the king had more affected the Duke of Albany than Cornwall.
It did always seem so to us, but now in the division of the kingdom, it appears not which of the dukes he values most.
Is not this your son, my lord?
His breeding, sir, hath been at my charge. I have so often blushed to acknowledge him that now I am brazed to it.

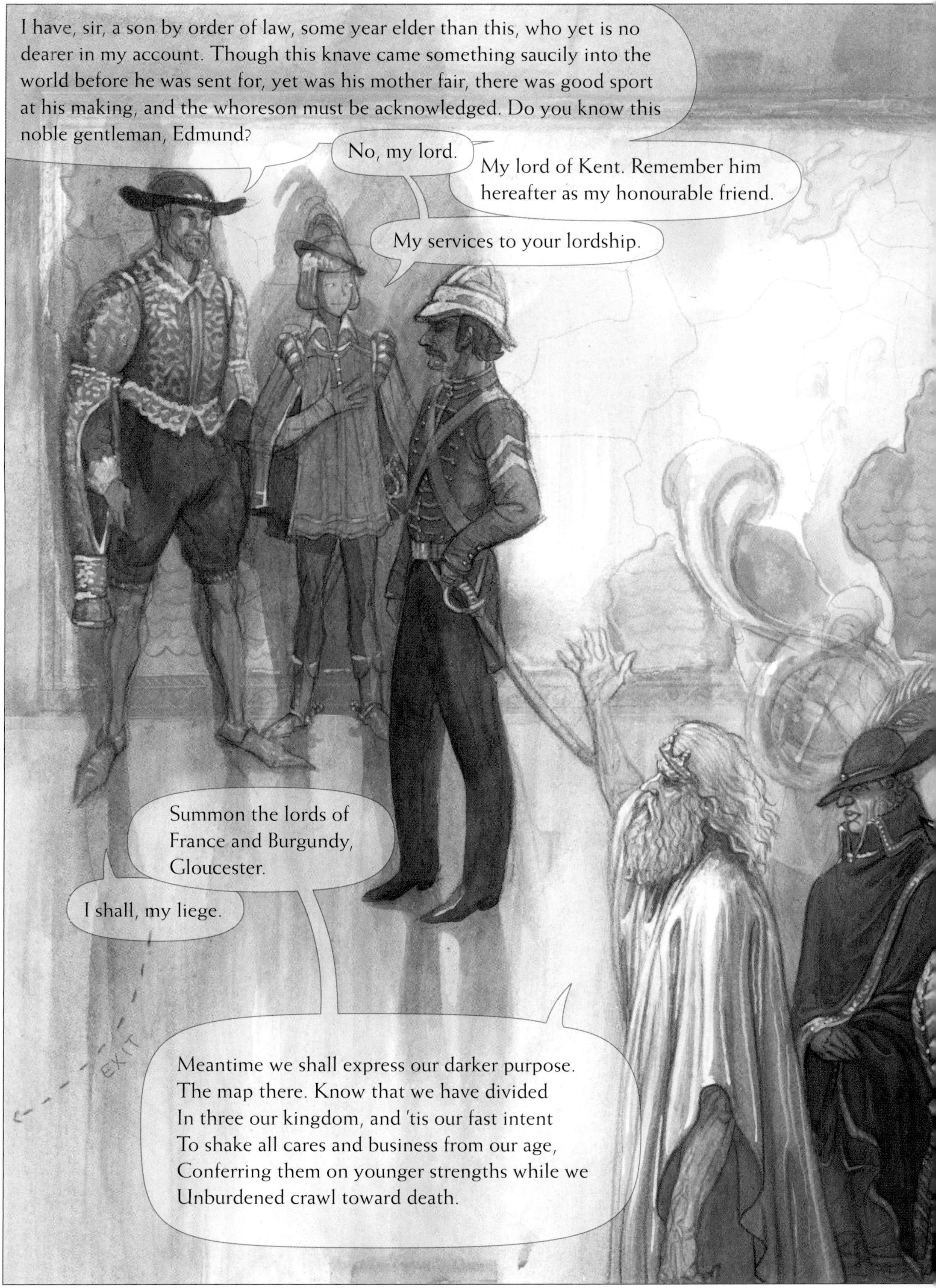
I have, sir, a son by order of law, some year elder than this, who yet is no dearer in my account. Though this knave came something saucily into the world before he was sent for, yet was his mother fair, there was good sport at his making, and the whoreson must be acknowledged. Do you know this noble gentleman, Edmund?
No, my lord.
My lord of Kent. Remember him hereafter as my honourable friend.
My services to your lordship.
Summon the lords of France and Burgundy, Gloucester.
I shall, my liege.
EXIT
Meantime we shall express our darker purpose.
The map there. Know that we have divided
In three our kingdom, and 'tis our fast intent
To shake all cares and business from our age,
Conferring them on younger strengths while we
Unburdened crawl toward death.

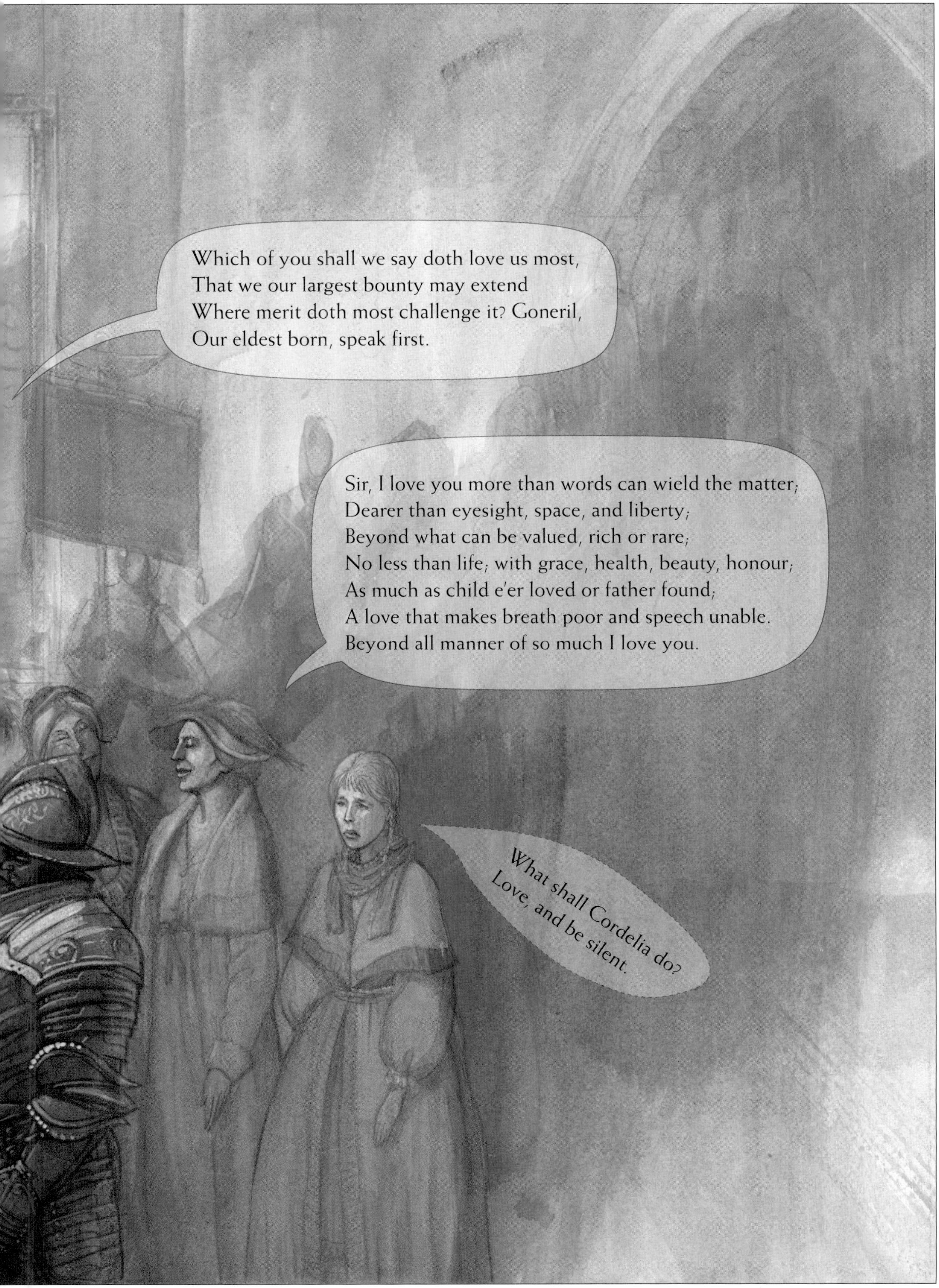
Which of you shall we say doth love us most,
That we our largest bounty may extend
Where merit doth most challenge it? Goneril,
Our eldest born, speak first.
Sir, I love you more than words can wield the matter;
Dearer than eyesight, space, and liberty;
Beyond what can be valued, rich or rare;
No less than life; with grace, health, beauty, honour;
As much as child e'er loved or father found;
A love that makes breath poor and speech unable.
Beyond all manner of so much I love you.
What shall Cordelia do?
Love, and be silent.

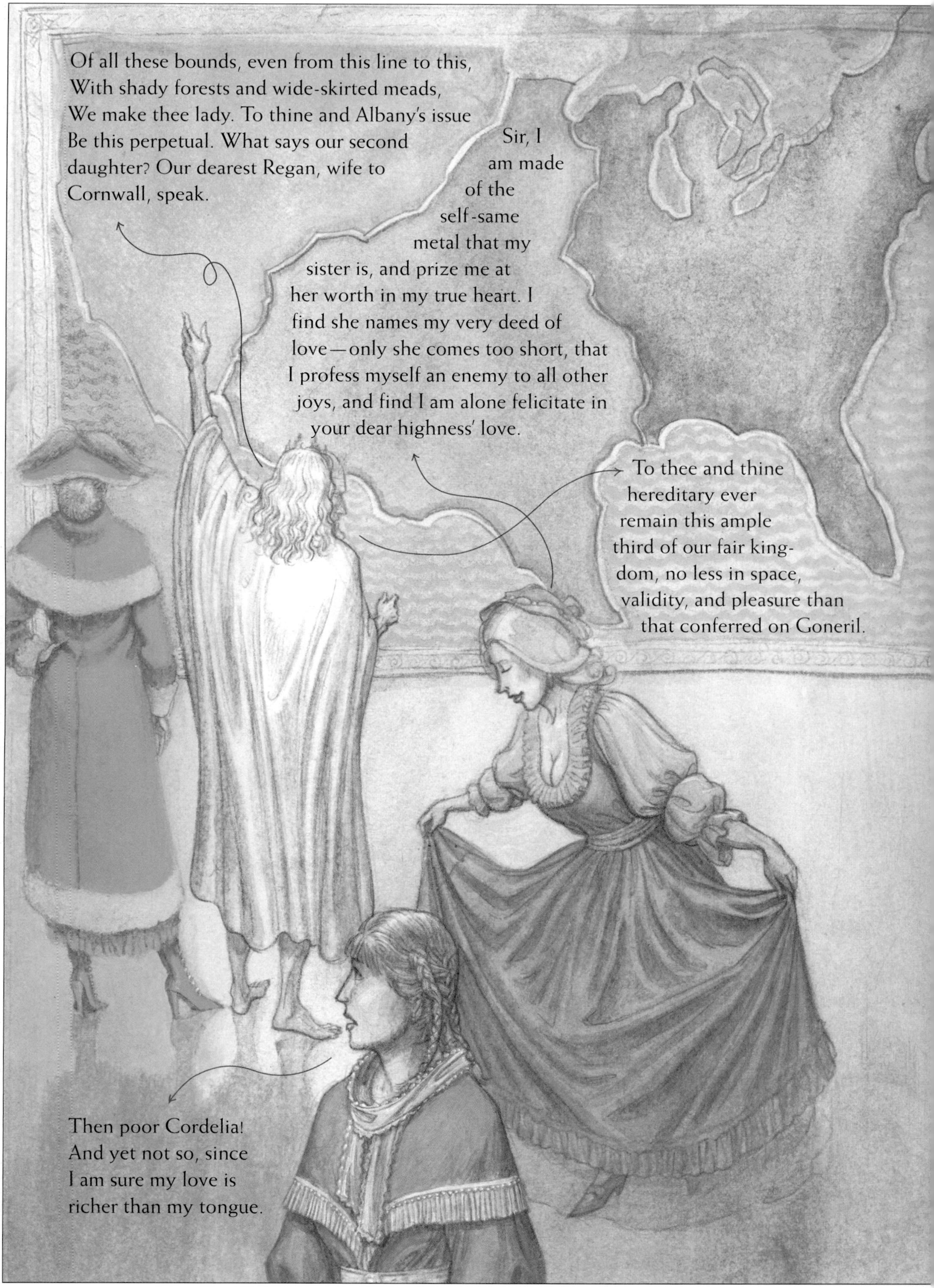
Of all these bounds, even from this line to this,
With shady forests and wide-skirted meads,
We make thee lady. To thine and Albany's issue
Be this perpetual. What says our second
daughter? Our dearest Regan, wife to
Cornwall, speak.
Sir, I am made of the self-same metal that my sister is, and prize me at her worth in my true heart. I find she names my very deed of love—only she comes too short, that I profess myself an enemy to all other joys, and find I am alone felicitate in your dear highness' love.
To thee and thine hereditary ever remain this ample third of our fair king-dom, no less in space, validity, and pleasure than that conferred on Goneril.
Then poor Cordelia! And yet not so, since I am sure my love is richer than my tongue.

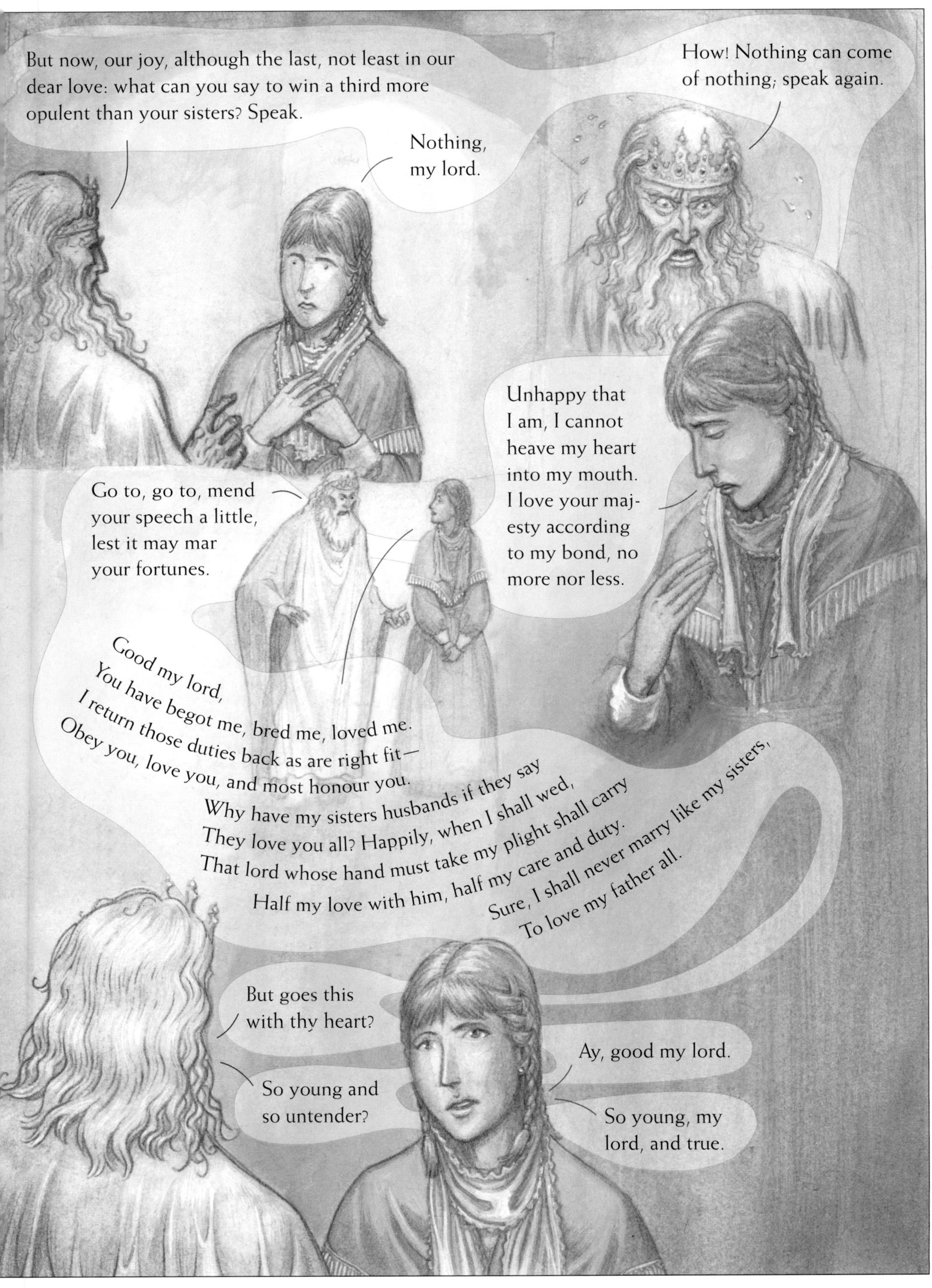
But now, our joy, although the last, not least in our dear love: what can you say to win a third more opulent than your sisters? Speak.
Nothing, my lord.
How! Nothing can come of nothing; speak again.
Unhappy that I am, I cannot heave my heart into my mouth. I love your majesty according to my bond, no more nor less.
Go to, go to, mend your speech a little, lest it may mar your fortunes.
Good my lord,
You have begot me, bred me, loved me.
I return those duties back as are right fit—
Obey you, love you, and most honour you.
Why have my sisters husbands if they say
They love you all? Happily, when I shall wed,
That lord whose hand must take my plight shall carry
Half my love with him, half my care and duty.
Sure, I shall never marry like my sisters,
To love my father all.
But goes this with thy heart?
Ay, good my lord.
So young and so untender?
So young, my lord, and true.

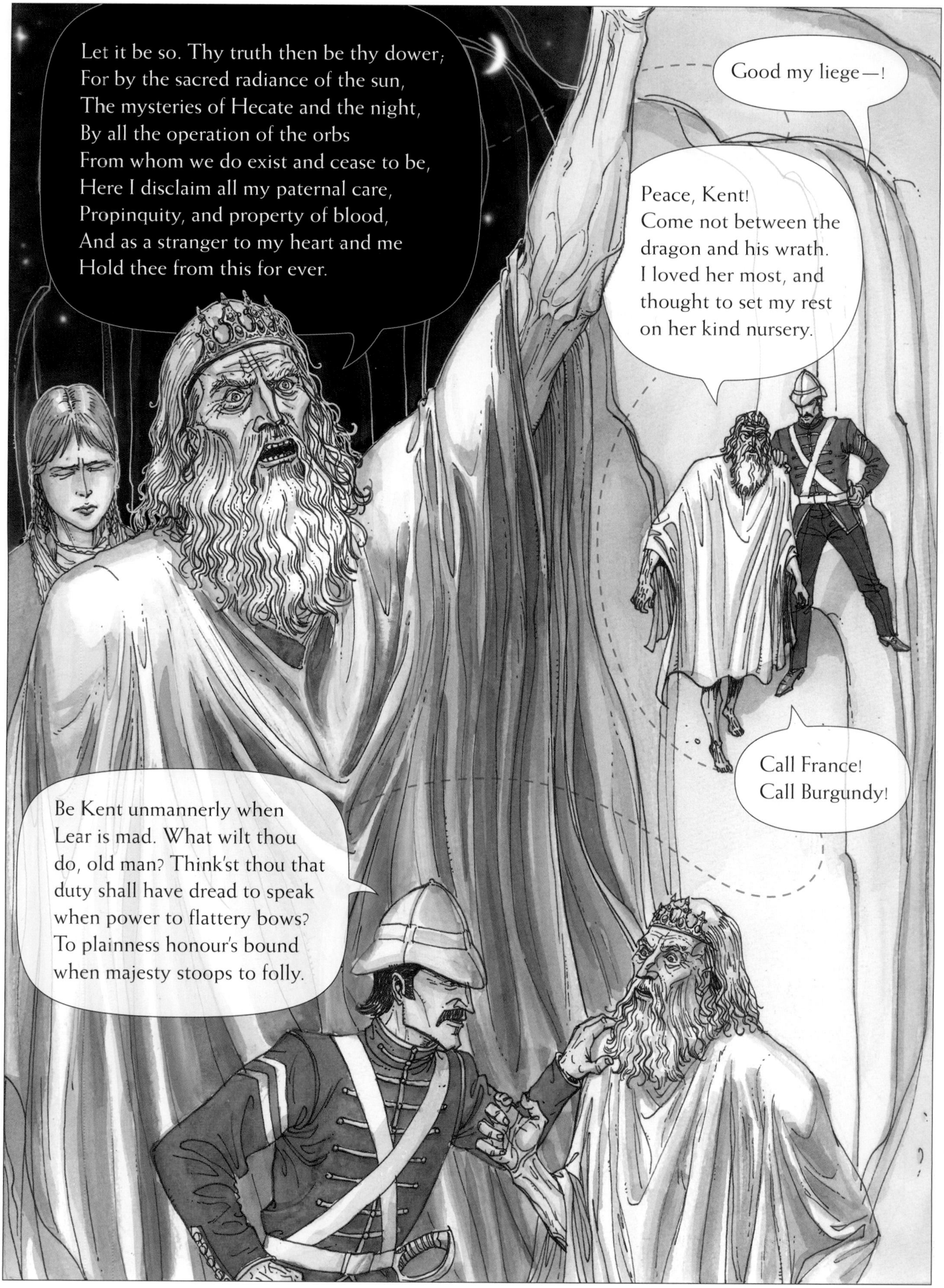
Let it be so. Thy truth then be thy dower;
For by the sacred radiance of the sun,
The mysteries of Hecate and the night,
By all the operation of the orbs
From whom we do exist and cease to be,
Here I disclaim all my paternal care,
Propinquity, and property of blood,
And as a stranger to my heart and me
Hold thee from this for ever.
Good my liege—!
Peace, Kent!
Come not between the dragon and his wrath.
I loved her most, and thought to set my rest on her kind nursery.
Call France!
Call Burgundy!
Be Kent unmannerly when Lear is mad. What wilt thou do, old man? Think'st thou that duty shall have dread to speak when power to flattery bows? To plainness honour's bound when majesty stoops to folly.

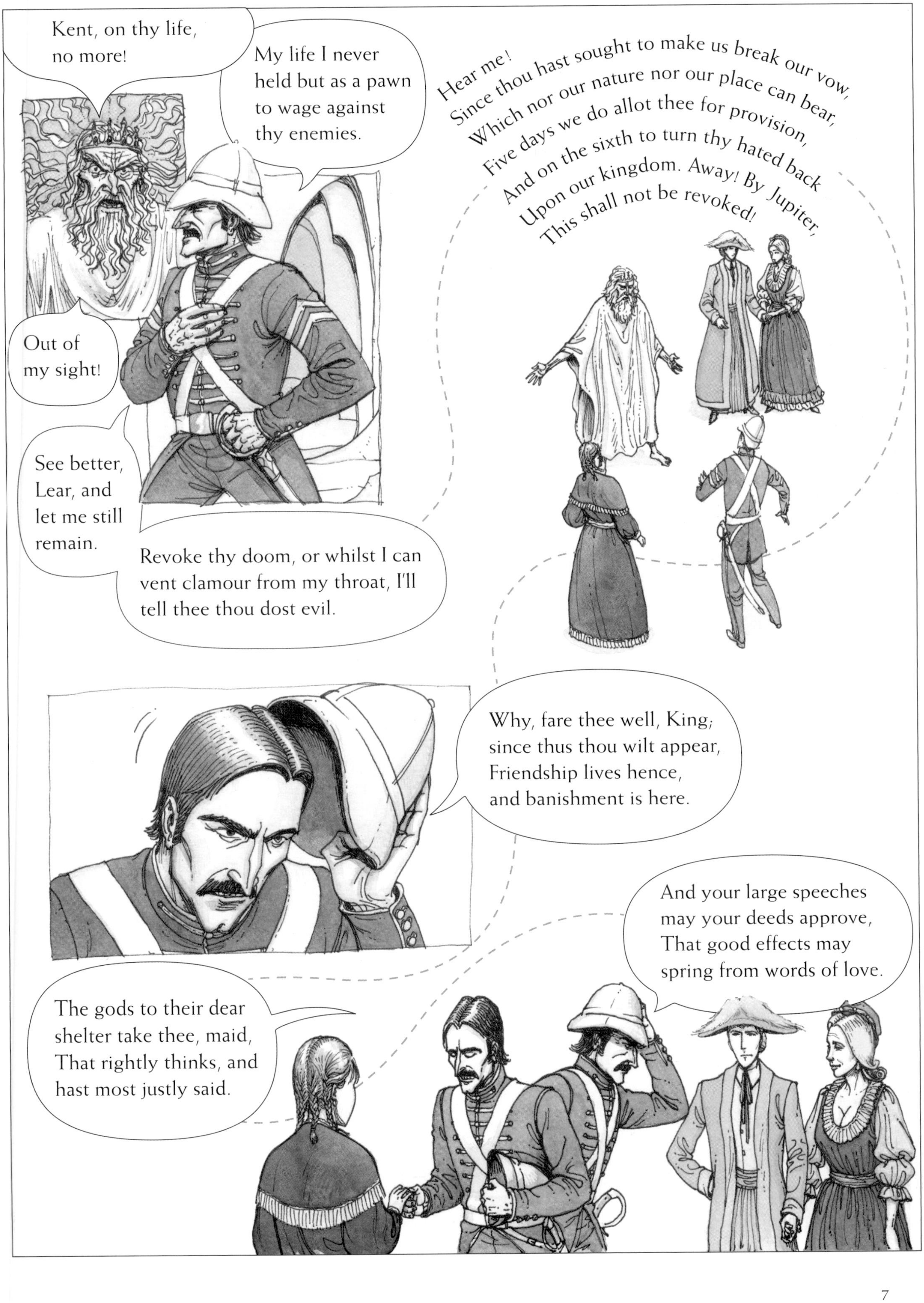

Kent, on thy life, no more!
My life I never held but as a pawn to wage against thy enemies.
Out of my sight!
See better, Lear, and let me still remain.
Revoke thy doom, or whilst I can vent clamour from my throat, I'll tell thee thou dost evil.
Hear me!
Since thou hast sought to make us break our vow,
Which nor our nature nor our place can bear,
Five days we do allot thee for provision,
And on the sixth to turn thy hated back
Upon our kingdom. Away! By Jupiter,
This shall not be revoked!
Why, fare thee well, King; since thus thou wilt appear, Friendship lives hence, and banishment is here.
The gods to their dear shelter take thee, maid, That rightly thinks, and hast most justly said.
And your large speeches may your deeds approve, That good effects may spring from words of love.

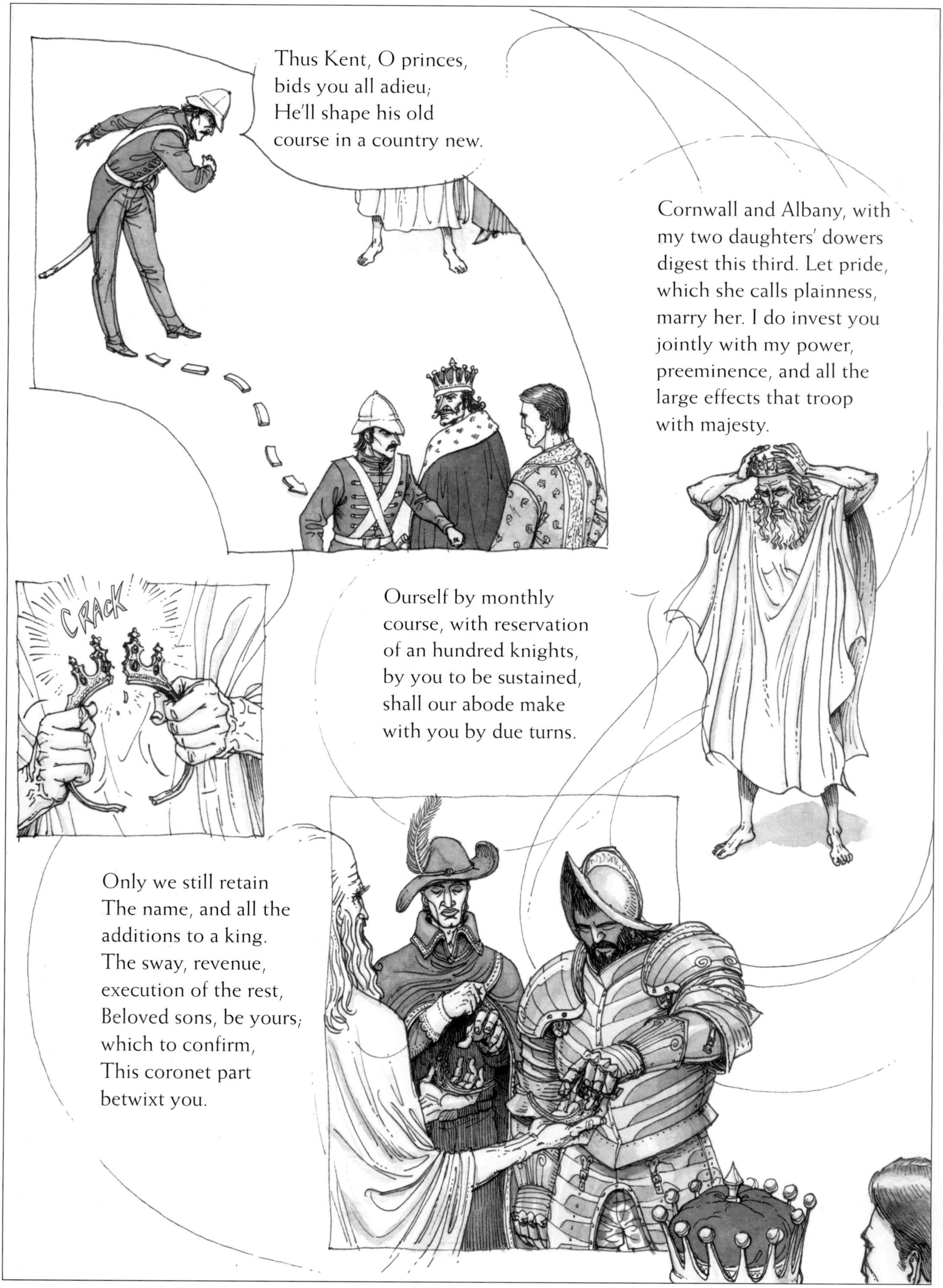
Thus Kent, O princes, bids you all adieu; He'll shape his old course in a country new.
Cornwall and Albany, with my two daughters' dowers digest this third. Let pride, which she calls plainness, marry her. I do invest you jointly with my power, preeminence, and all the large effects that troop with majesty.
CRACK
Ourself by monthly course, with reservation of an hundred knights, by you to be sustained, shall our abode make with you by due turns.
Only we still retain The name, and all the additions to a king. The sway, revenue, execution of the rest, Beloved sons, be yours; which to confirm, This coronet part betwixt you.

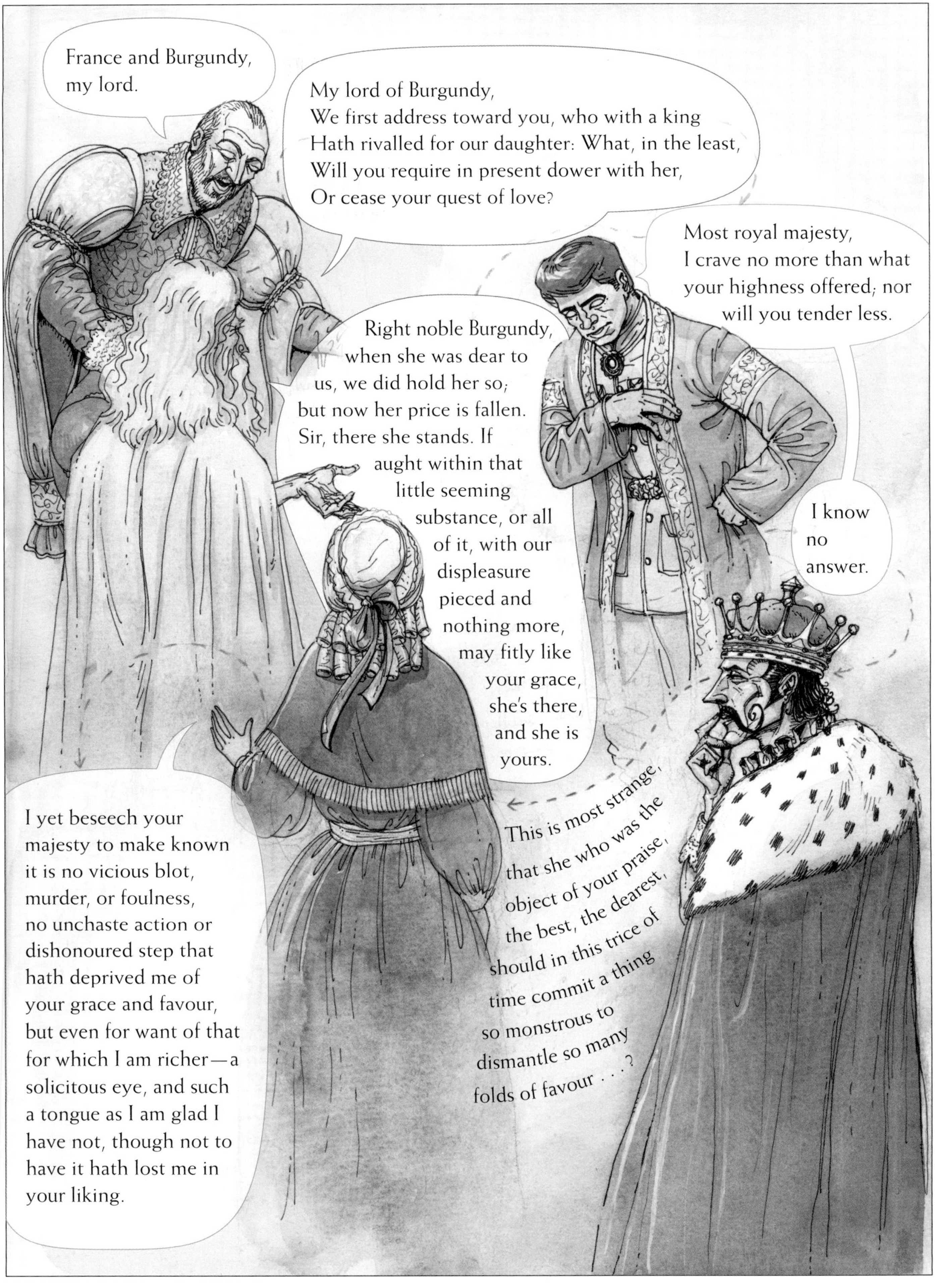
France and Burgundy, my lord.
My lord of Burgundy, We first address toward you, who with a king Hath rivalled for our daughter: What, in the least, Will you require in present dower with her, Or cease your quest of love?
Most royal majesty, I crave no more than what your highness offered; nor will you tender less.
Right noble Burgundy, when she was dear to us, we did hold her so; but now her price is fallen. Sir, there she stands. If aught within that little seeming substance, or all of it, with our displeasure pieced and nothing more, may fitly like your grace, she's there, and she is yours.
I know no answer.
I yet beseech your majesty to make known it is no vicious blot, murder, or foulness, no unchaste action or dishonoured step that hath deprived me of your grace and favour, but even for want of that for which I am richer—a solicitous eye, and such a tongue as I am glad I have not, though not to have it hath lost me in your liking.
This is most strange, that she who was the object of your praise, the best, the dearest, should in this trice of time commit a thing so monstrous to dismantle so many folds of favour . . . ?

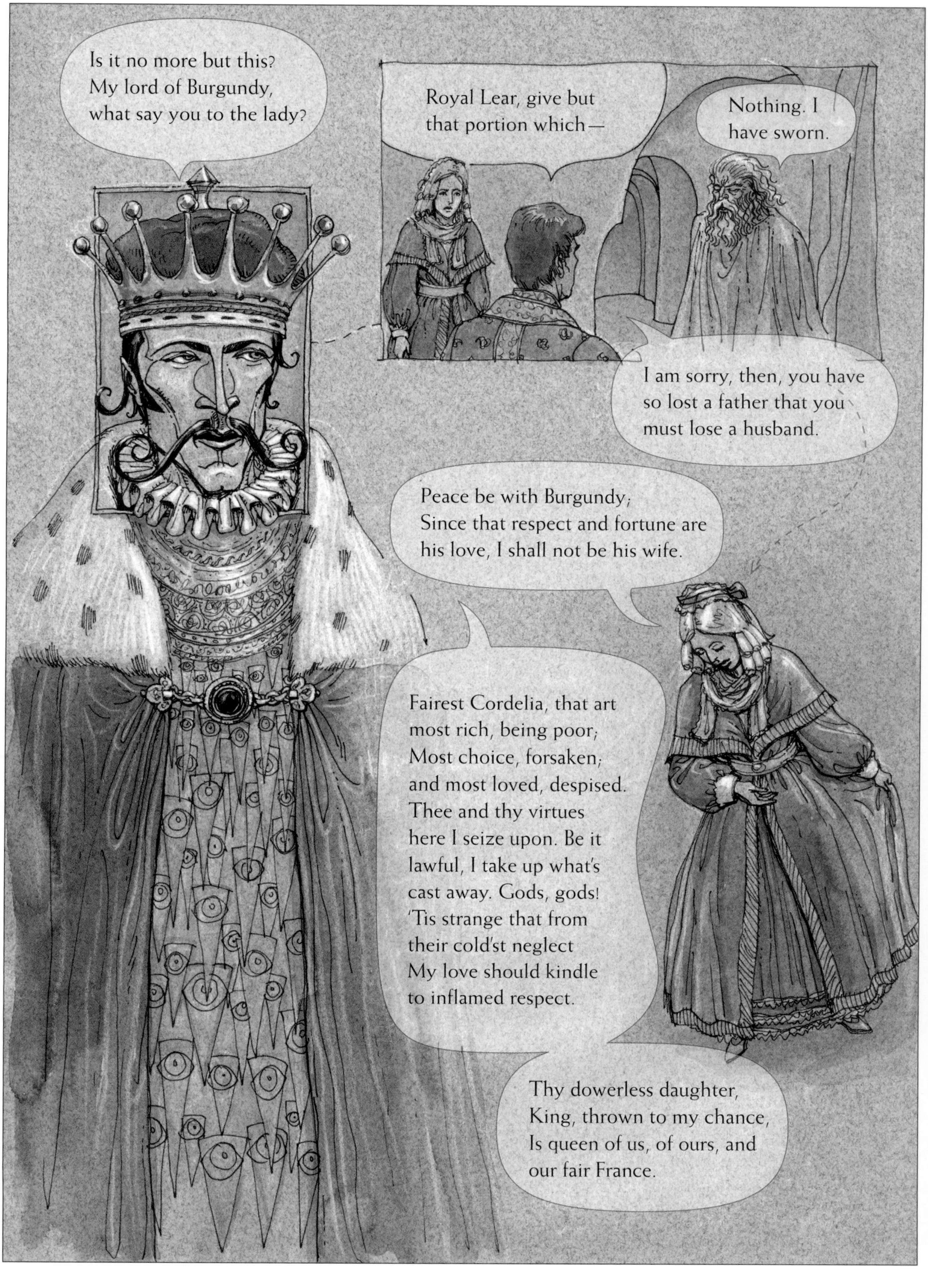
Is it no more but this? My lord of Burgundy, what say you to the lady?
Royal Lear, give but that portion which—
Nothing. I have sworn.
I am sorry, then, you have so lost a father that you must lose a husband.
Peace be with Burgundy; Since that respect and fortune are his love, I shall not be his wife.
Fairest Cordelia, that art most rich, being poor; Most choice, forsaken; and most loved, despised. Thee and thy virtues here I seize upon. Be it lawful, I take up what's cast away. Gods, gods! 'Tis strange that from their cold'st neglect My love should kindle to inflamed respect.
Thy dowerless daughter, King, thrown to my chance, Is queen of us, of ours, and our fair France.

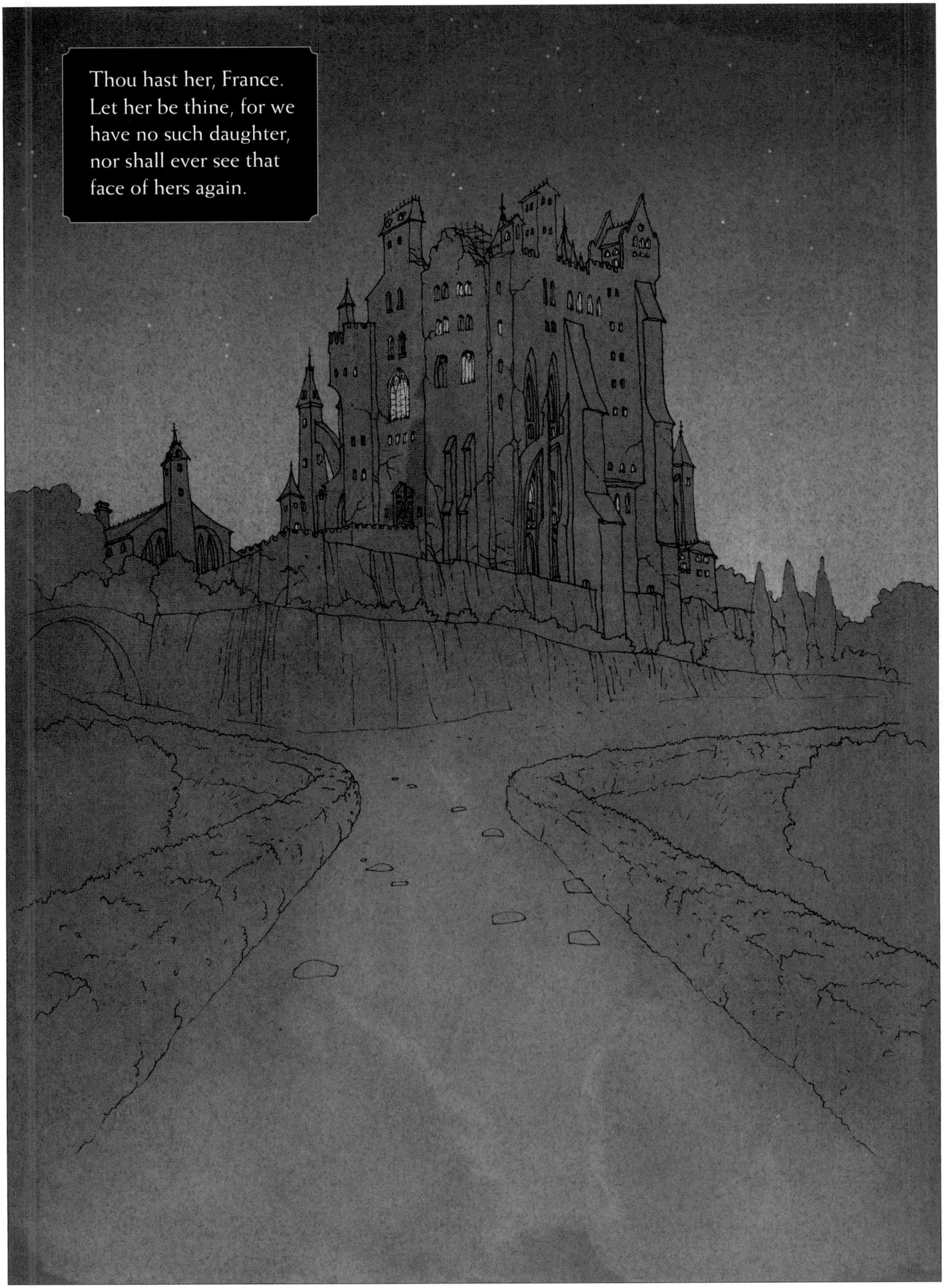
Thou hast her, France. Let her be thine, for we have no such daughter, nor shall ever see that face of hers again.

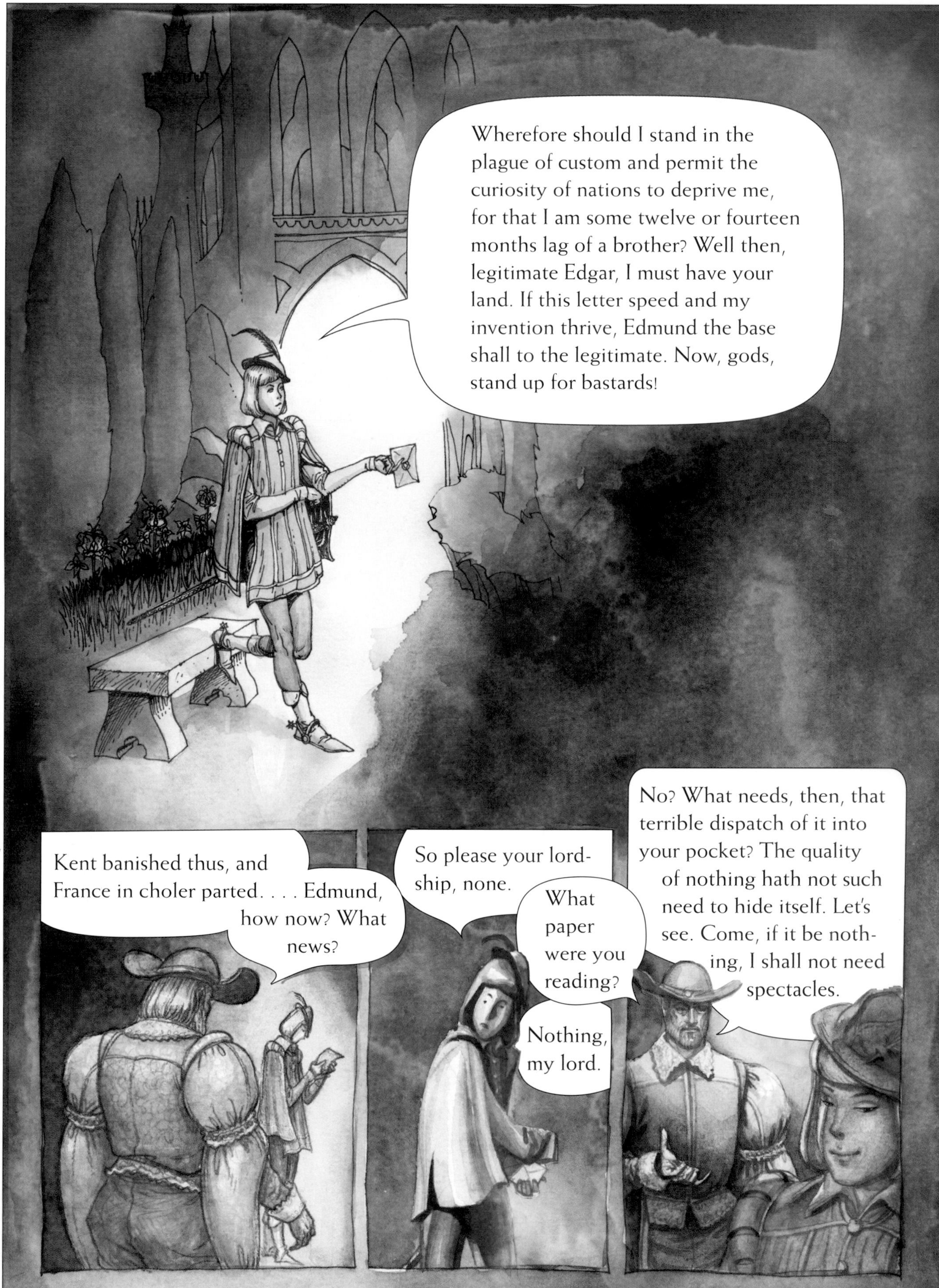
Wherefore should I stand in the plague of custom and permit the curiosity of nations to deprive me, for that I am some twelve or fourteen months lag of a brother? Well then, legitimate Edgar, I must have your land. If this letter speed and my invention thrive, Edmund the base shall to the legitimate. Now, gods, stand up for bastards!
Kent banished thus, and France in choler parted. . . . Edmund, how now? What news?
So please your lordship, none.
What paper were you reading?
Nothing, my lord.
No? What needs, then, that terrible dispatch of it into your pocket? The quality of nothing hath not such need to hide itself. Let's see. Come, if it be nothing, I shall not need spectacles.

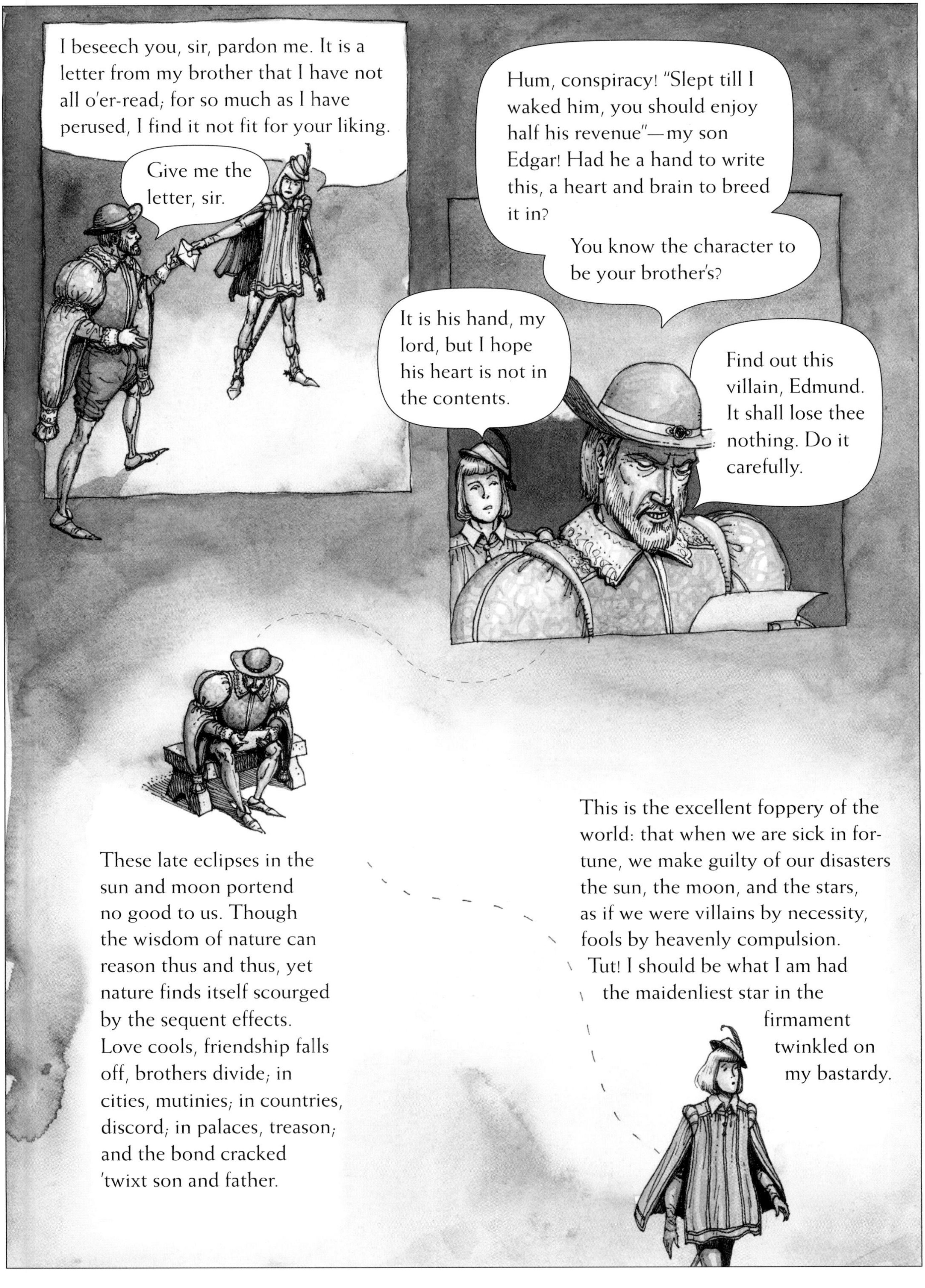
I beseech you, sir, pardon me. It is a letter from my brother that I have not all o'er-read; for so much as I have perused, I find it not fit for your liking.
Give me the letter, sir.
Hum, conspiracy! "Slept till I waked him, you should enjoy half his revenue"—my son Edgar! Had he a hand to write this, a heart and brain to breed it in?
You know the character to be your brother's?
It is his hand, my lord, but I hope his heart is not in the contents.
Find out this villain, Edmund. It shall lose thee nothing. Do it carefully.
These late eclipses in the sun and moon portend no good to us. Though the wisdom of nature can reason thus and thus, yet nature finds itself scourged by the sequent effects. Love cools, friendship falls off, brothers divide; in cities, mutinies; in countries, discord; in palaces, treason; and the bond cracked 'twixt son and father.
This is the excellent foppery of the world: that when we are sick in fortune, we make guilty of our disasters the sun, the moon, and the stars, as if we were villains by necessity, fools by heavenly compulsion. Tut! I should be what I am had the maidenliest star in the firmament twinkled on my bastardy.

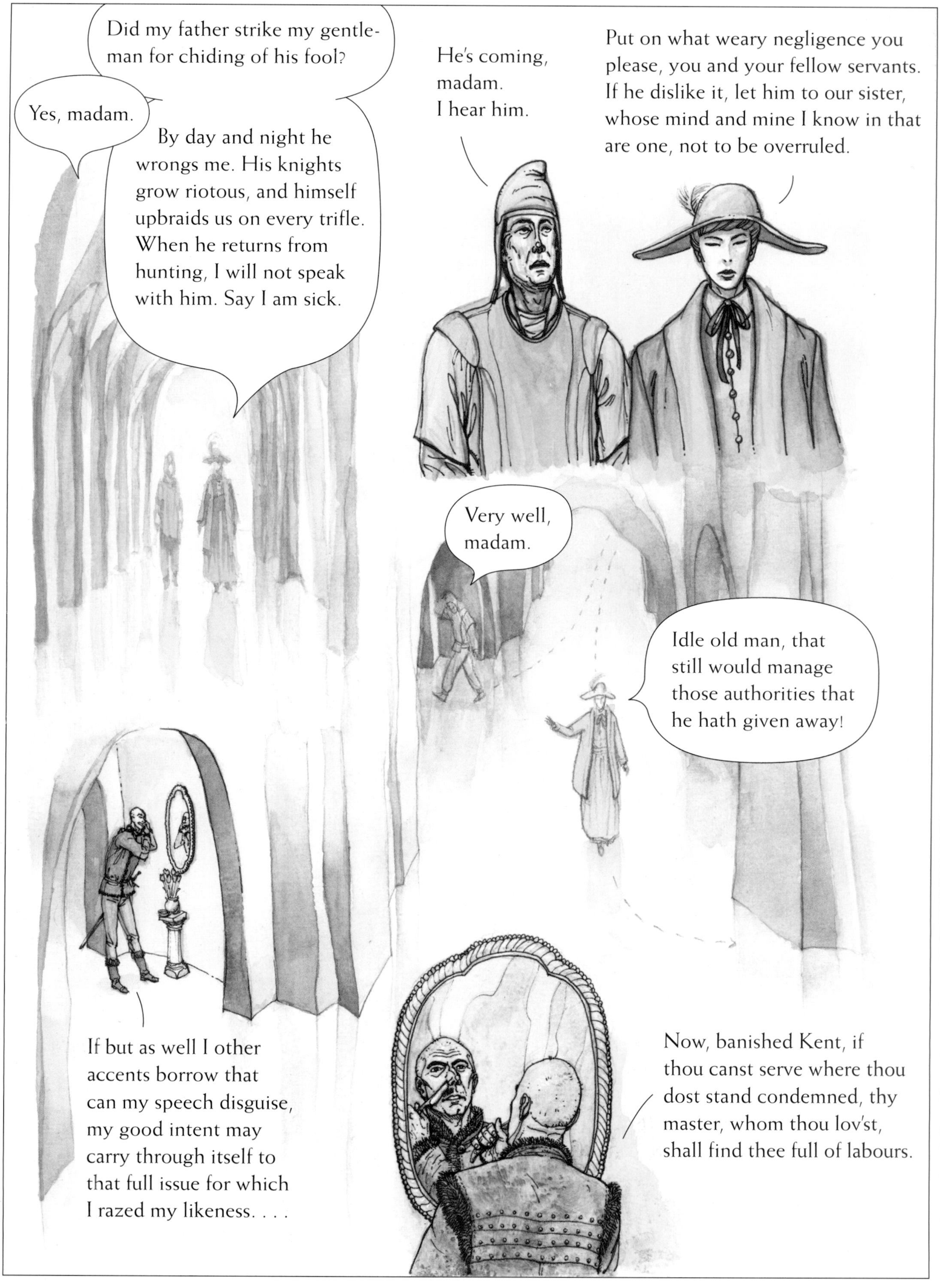
Did my father strike my gentleman for chiding of his fool?
Yes, madam.
By day and night he wrongs me. His knights grow riotous, and himself upbraids us on every trifle. When he returns from hunting, I will not speak with him. Say I am sick.
He's coming, madam. I hear him.
Put on what weary negligence you please, you and your fellow servants. If he dislike it, let him to our sister, whose mind and mine I know in that are one, not to be overruled.
Very well, madam.
Idle old man, that still would manage those authorities that he hath given away!
If but as well I other accents borrow that can my speech disguise, my good intent may carry through itself to that full issue for which I razed my likeness. . . .
Now, banished Kent, if thou canst serve where thou dost stand condemned, thy master, whom thou lov'st, shall find thee full of labours.

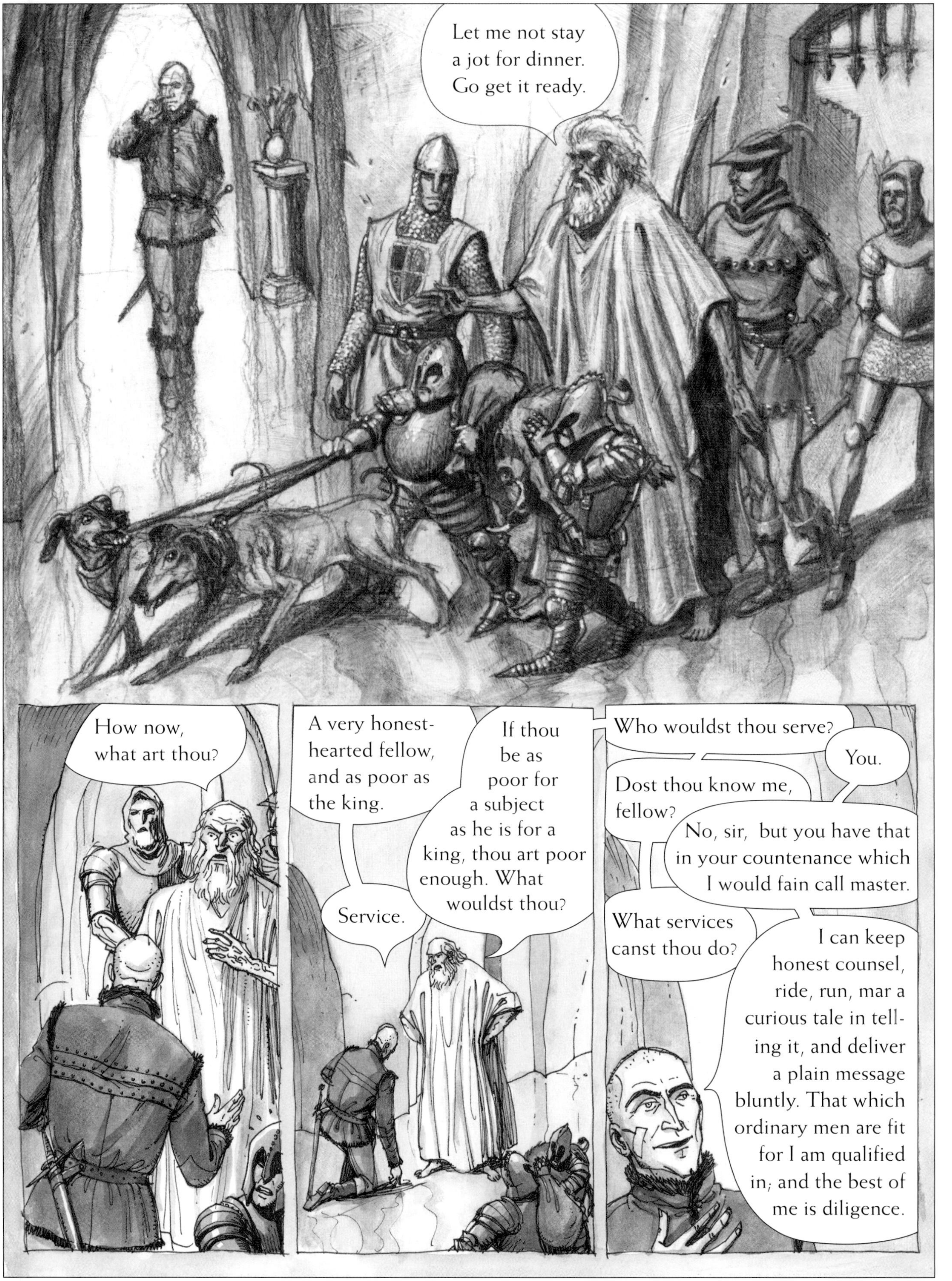
Let me not stay a jot for dinner. Go get it ready.
How now, what art thou?
A very honest-hearted fellow, and as poor as the king.
If thou be as poor for a subject as he is for a king, thou art poor enough. What wouldst thou?
Service.
Who wouldst thou serve?
You.
Dost thou know me, fellow?
No, sir, but you have that in your countenance which I would fain call master.
What services canst thou do?
I can keep honest counsel, ride, run, mar a curious tale in telling it, and deliver a plain message bluntly. That which ordinary men are fit for I am qualified in; and the best of me is diligence.

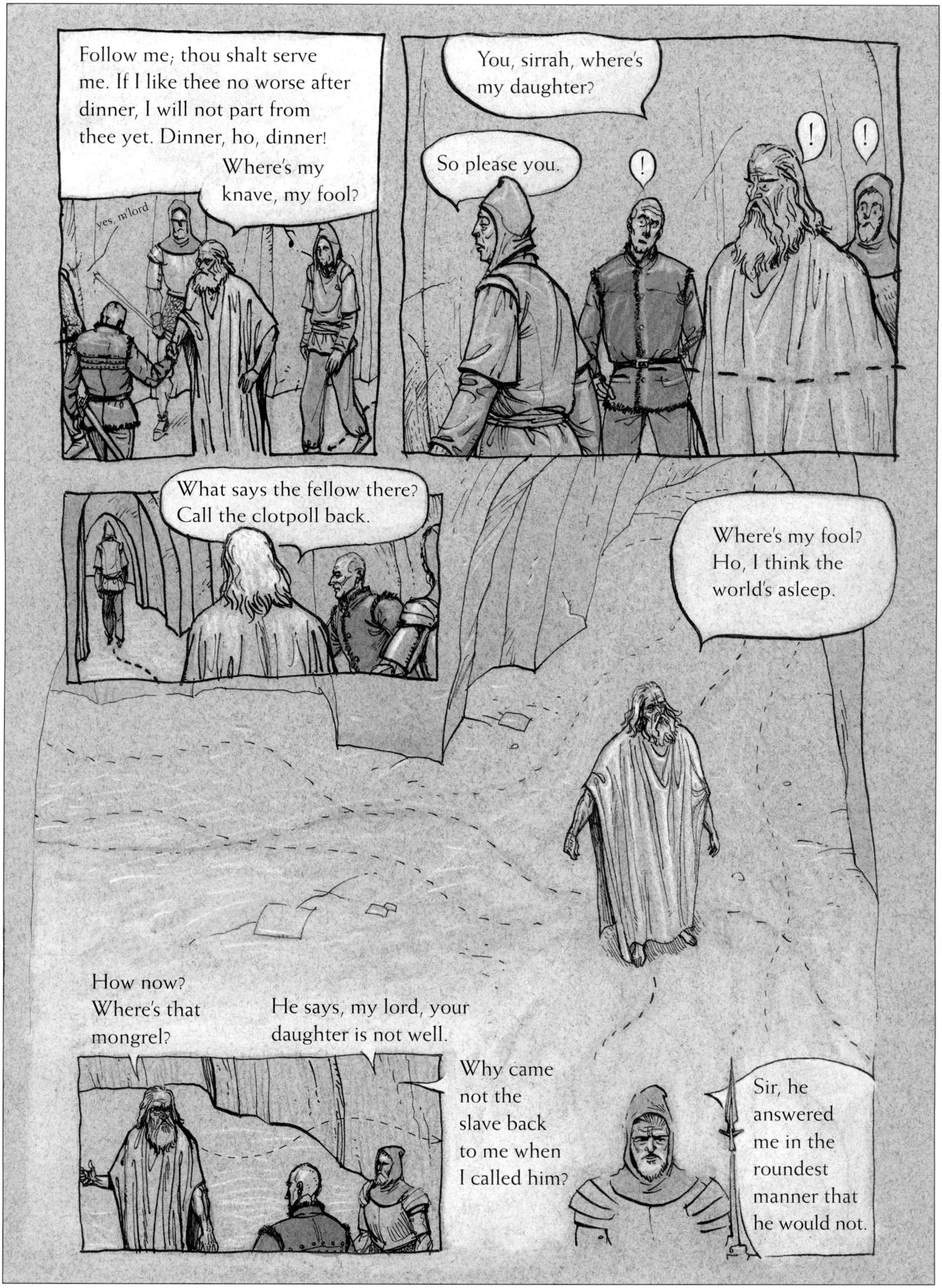
Follow me; thou shalt serve me. If I like thee no worse after dinner, I will not part from thee yet. Dinner, ho, dinner!
Where's my knave, my fool?
yes, m'lord
You, sirrah, where's my daughter?
So please you.
!
!
!
What says the fellow there? Call the clotpoll back.
Where's my fool? Ho, I think the world's asleep.
How now? Where's that mongrel?
He says, my lord, your daughter is not well.
Why came not the slave back to me when I called him?
Sir, he answered me in the roundest manner that he would not.

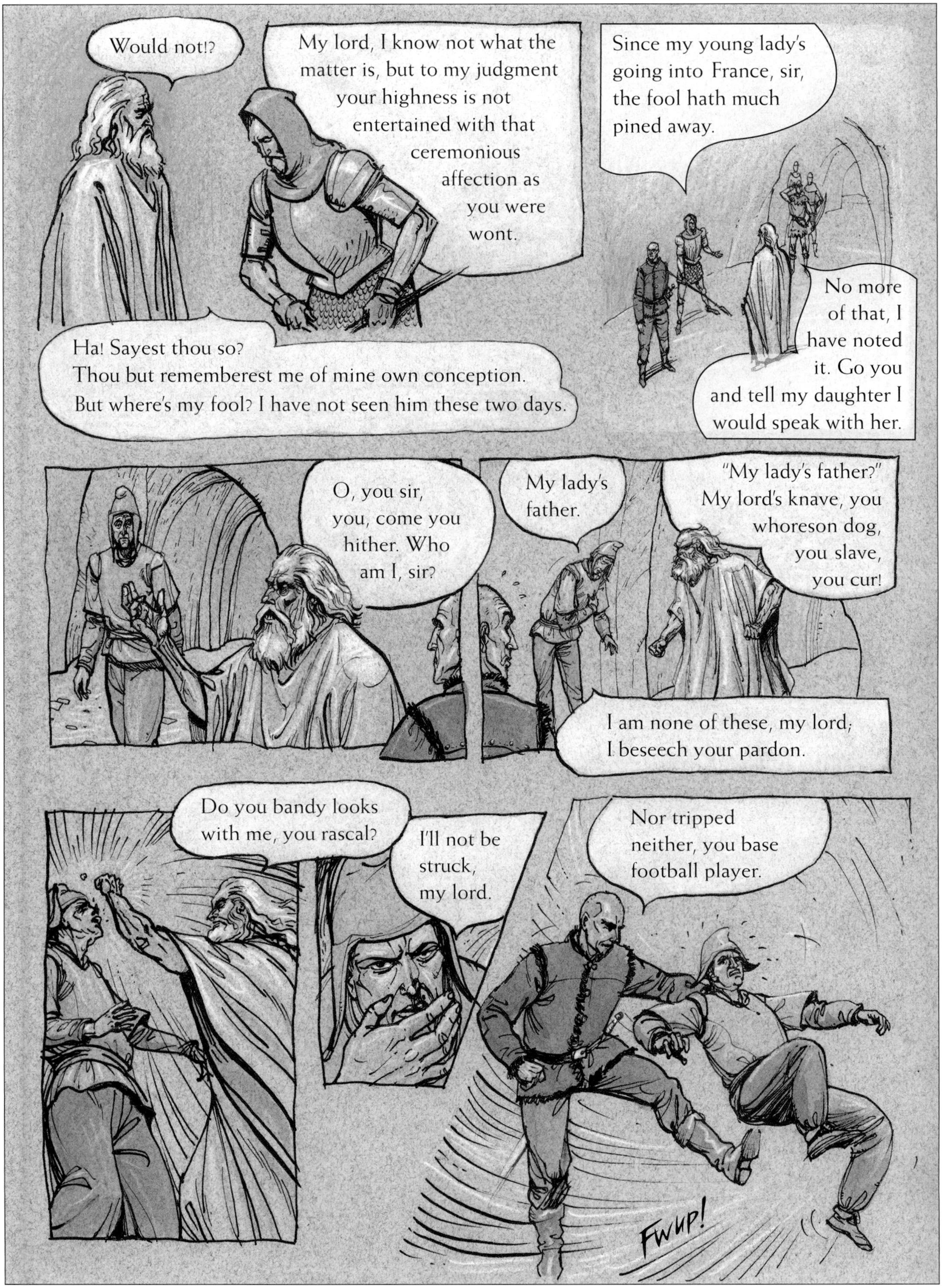
Would not!?
My lord, I know not what the matter is, but to my judgment your highness is not entertained with that ceremonious affection as you were wont.
Ha! Sayest thou so?
Thou but rememberest me of mine own conception.
But where's my fool? I have not seen him these two days.
Since my young lady's going into France, sir, the fool hath much pined away.
No more of that, I have noted it. Go you and tell my daughter I would speak with her.
O, you sir, you, come you hither. Who am I, sir?
My lady's father.
"My lady's father?" My lord's knave, you whoreson dog, you slave, you cur!
I am none of these, my lord; I beseech your pardon.
Do you bandy looks with me, you rascal?
I'll not be struck, my lord.
Nor tripped neither, you base football player.
FWUP!

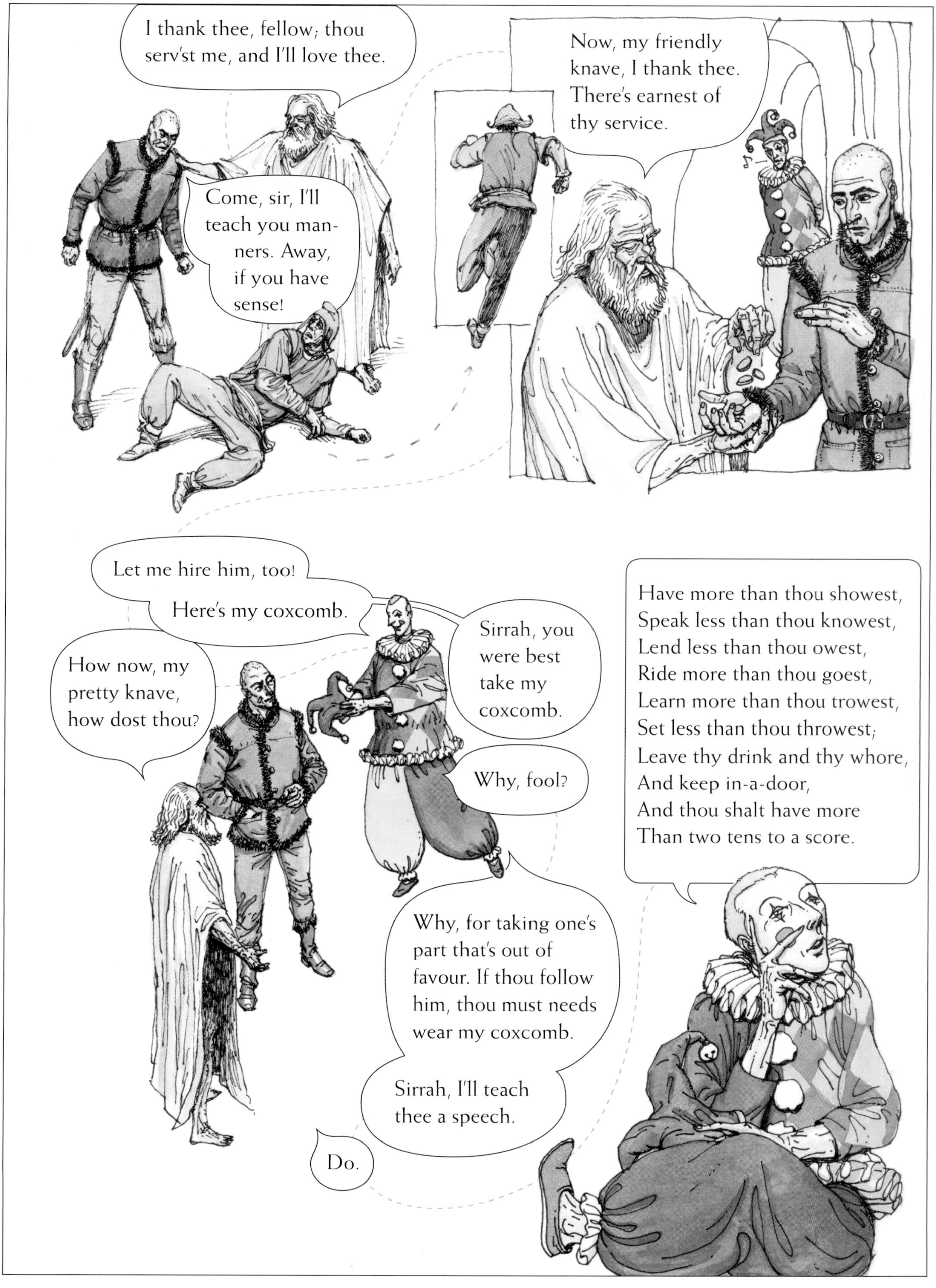
I thank thee, fellow; thou serv'st me, and I'll love thee.
Come, sir, I'll teach you manners. Away, if you have sense!
Now, my friendly knave, I thank thee. There's earnest of thy service.
Let me hire him, too!
Here's my coxcomb.
How now, my pretty knave, how dost thou?
Sirrah, you were best take my coxcomb.
Why, fool?
Why, for taking one's part that's out of favour. If thou follow him, thou must needs wear my coxcomb.
Sirrah, I'll teach thee a speech.
Do.
Have more than thou showest,
Speak less than thou knowest,
Lend less than thou owest,
Ride more than thou goest,
Learn more than thou trowest,
Set less than thou throwest;
Leave thy drink and thy whore,
And keep in-a-door,
And thou shalt have more
Than two tens to a score.

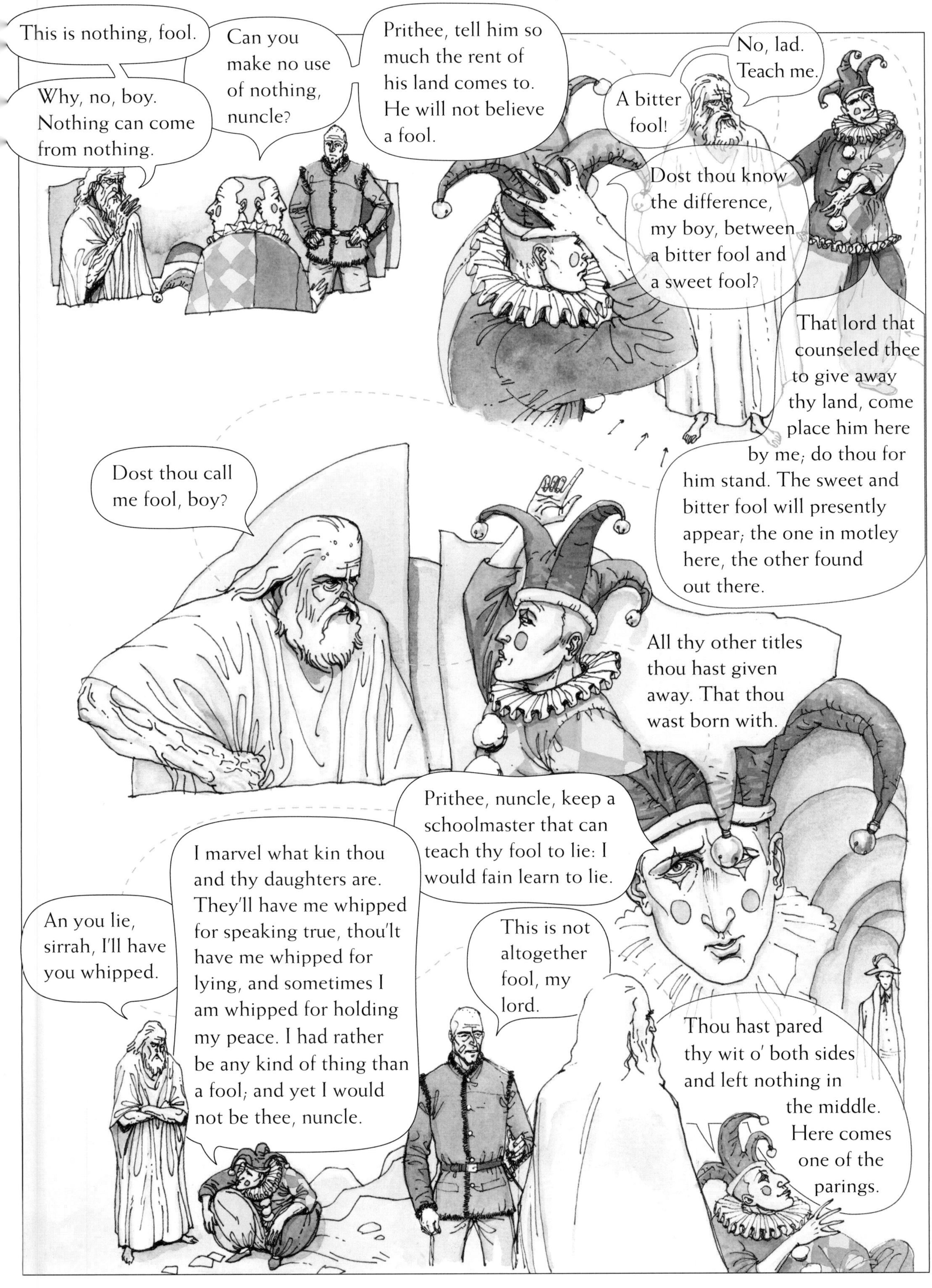
This is nothing, fool.
Can you make no use of nothing, nuncle?
Why, no, boy. Nothing can come from nothing.
Prithee, tell him so much the rent of his land comes to. He will not believe a fool.
A bitter fool!
No, lad. Teach me.
Dost thou know the difference, my boy, between a bitter fool and a sweet fool?
That lord that counseled thee to give away thy land, come place him here by me; do thou for him stand. The sweet and bitter fool will presently appear; the one in motley here, the other found out there.
Dost thou call me fool, boy?
All thy other titles thou hast given away. That thou wast born with.
This is not altogether fool, my lord.
Prithee, nuncle, keep a schoolmaster that can teach thy fool to lie: I would fain learn to lie.
An you lie, sirrah, I'll have you whipped.
I marvel what kin thou and thy daughters are. They'll have me whipped for speaking true, thou'lt have me whipped for lying, and sometimes I am whipped for holding my peace. I had rather be any kind of thing than a fool; and yet I would not be thee, nuncle.
Thou hast pared thy wit o' both sides and left nothing in the middle. Here comes one of the parings.

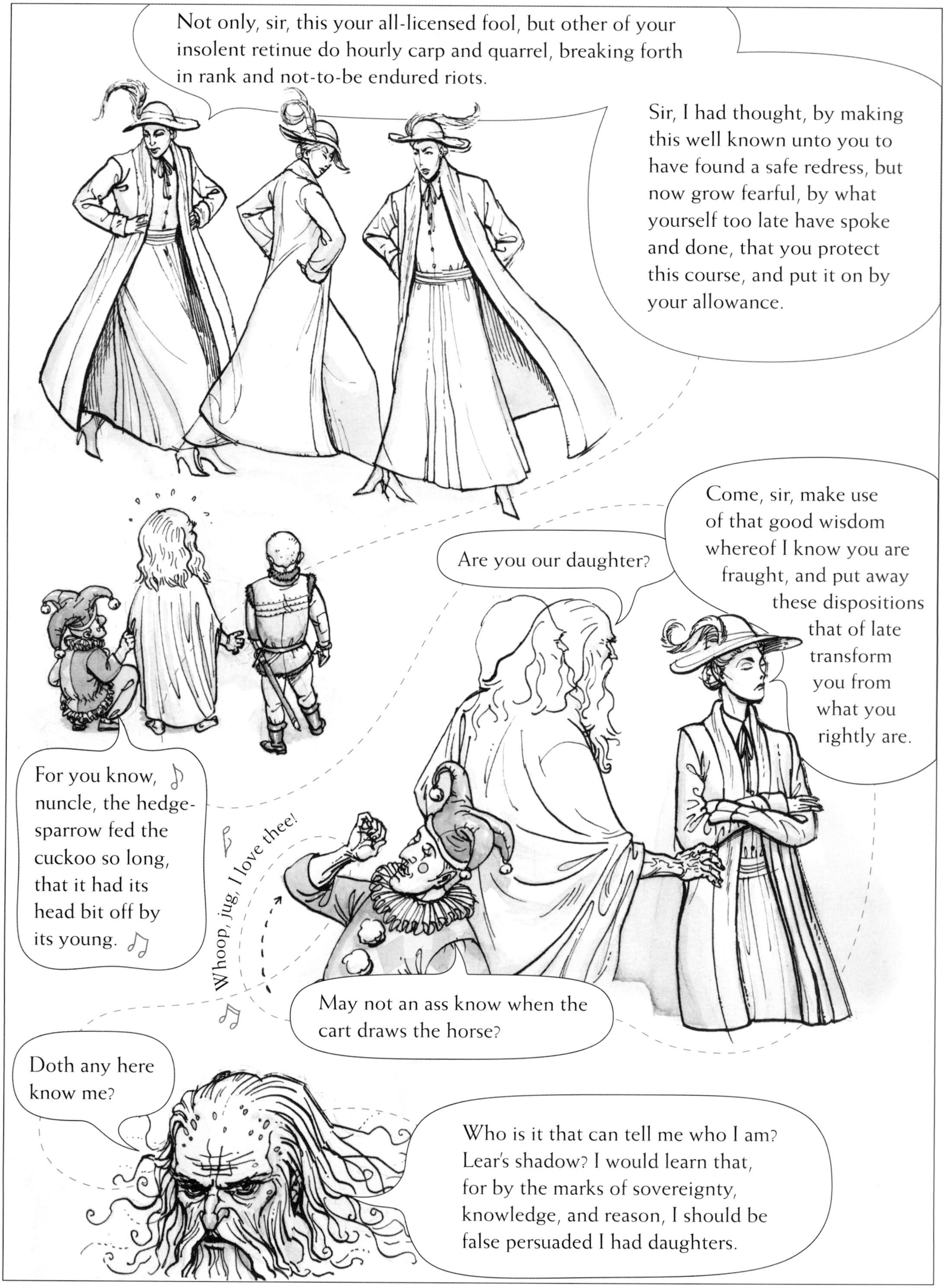
Not only, sir, this your all-licensed fool, but other of your insolent retinue do hourly carp and quarrel, breaking forth in rank and not-to-be endured riots.
Sir, I had thought, by making this well known unto you to have found a safe redress, but now grow fearful, by what yourself too late have spoke and done, that you protect this course, and put it on by your allowance.
Are you our daughter?
Come, sir, make use of that good wisdom whereof I know you are fraught, and put away these dispositions that of late transform you from what you rightly are.
For you know, nuncle, the hedge-sparrow fed the cuckoo so long, that it had its head bit off by its young.
Whoop, jug, I love thee!
May not an ass know when the cart draws the horse?
Doth any here know me?
Who is it that can tell me who I am? Lear's shadow? I would learn that, for by the marks of sovereignty, knowledge, and reason, I should be false persuaded I had daughters.

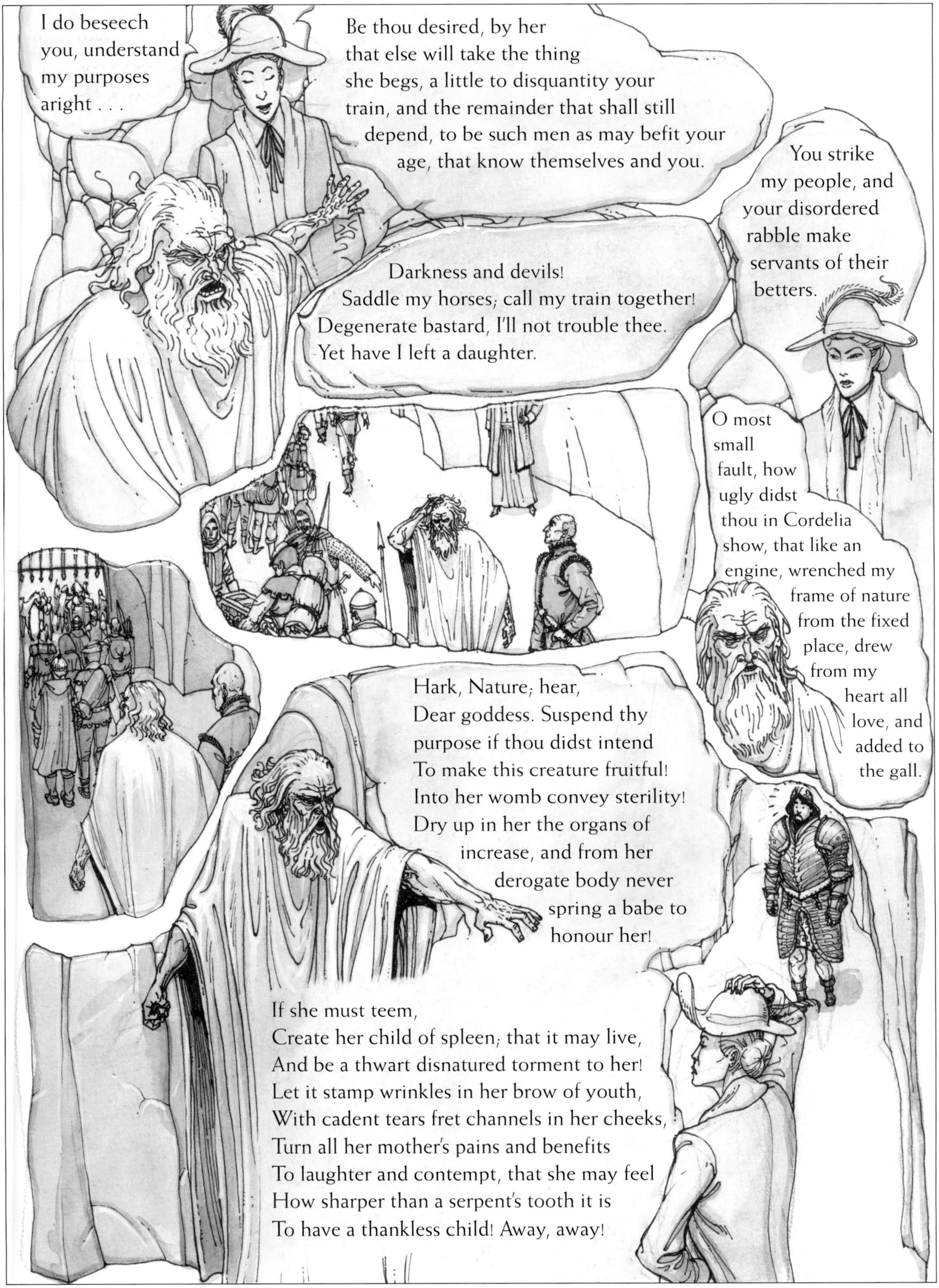
I do beseech you, understand my purposes aright . . .
Be thou desired, by her that else will take the thing she begs, a little to disquantity your train, and the remainder that shall still depend, to be such men as may befit your age, that know themselves and you.
You strike my people, and your disordered rabble make servants of their betters.
Darkness and devils! Saddle my horses; call my train together! Degenerate bastard, I'll not trouble thee. Yet have I left a daughter.
O most small fault, how ugly didst thou in Cordelia show, that like an engine, wrenched my frame of nature from the fixed place, drew from my heart all love, and added to the gall.
Hark, Nature; hear, Dear goddess. Suspend thy purpose if thou didst intend To make this creature fruitful! Into her womb convey sterility! Dry up in her the organs of increase, and from her derogate body never spring a babe to honour her!
If she must teem, Create her child of spleen; that it may live, And be a thwart disnatured torment to her! Let it stamp wrinkles in her brow of youth, With cadent tears fret channels in her cheeks, Turn all her mother's pains and benefits To laughter and contempt, that she may feel How sharper than a serpent's tooth it is To have a thankless child! Away, away!

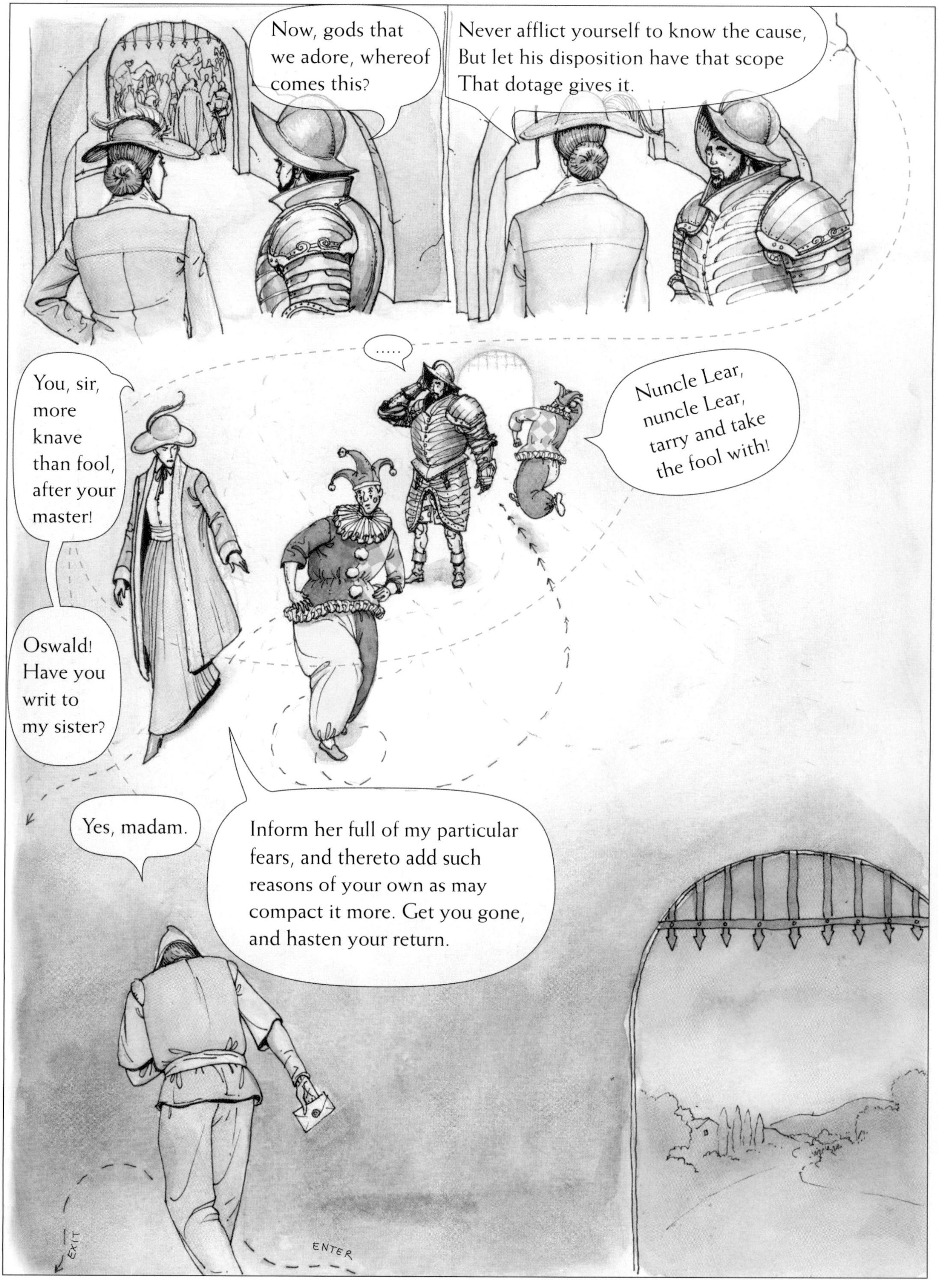
Now, gods that we adore, whereof comes this?
Never afflict yourself to know the cause, But let his disposition have that scope That dotage gives it.
.....
You, sir, more knave than fool, after your master!
Nuncle Lear, nuncle Lear, tarry and take the fool with!
Oswald! Have you writ to my sister?
Yes, madam.
Inform her full of my particular fears, and thereto add such reasons of your own as may compact it more. Get you gone, and hasten your return.
EXIT
ENTER

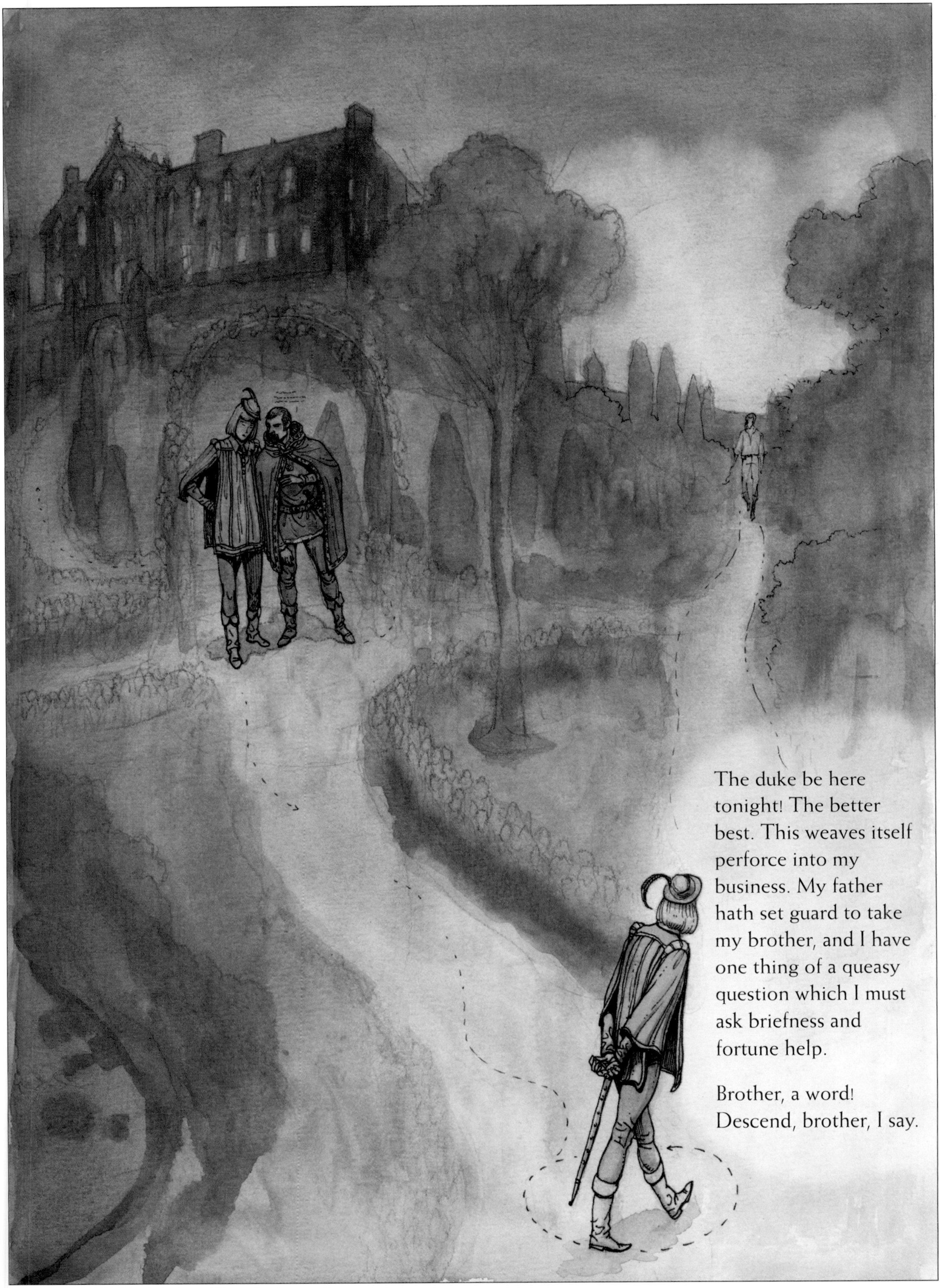

The duke be here tonight! The better best. This weaves itself perforce into my business. My father hath set guard to take my brother, and I have one thing of a queasy question which I must ask briefness and fortune help.

Brother, a word! Descend, brother, I say.

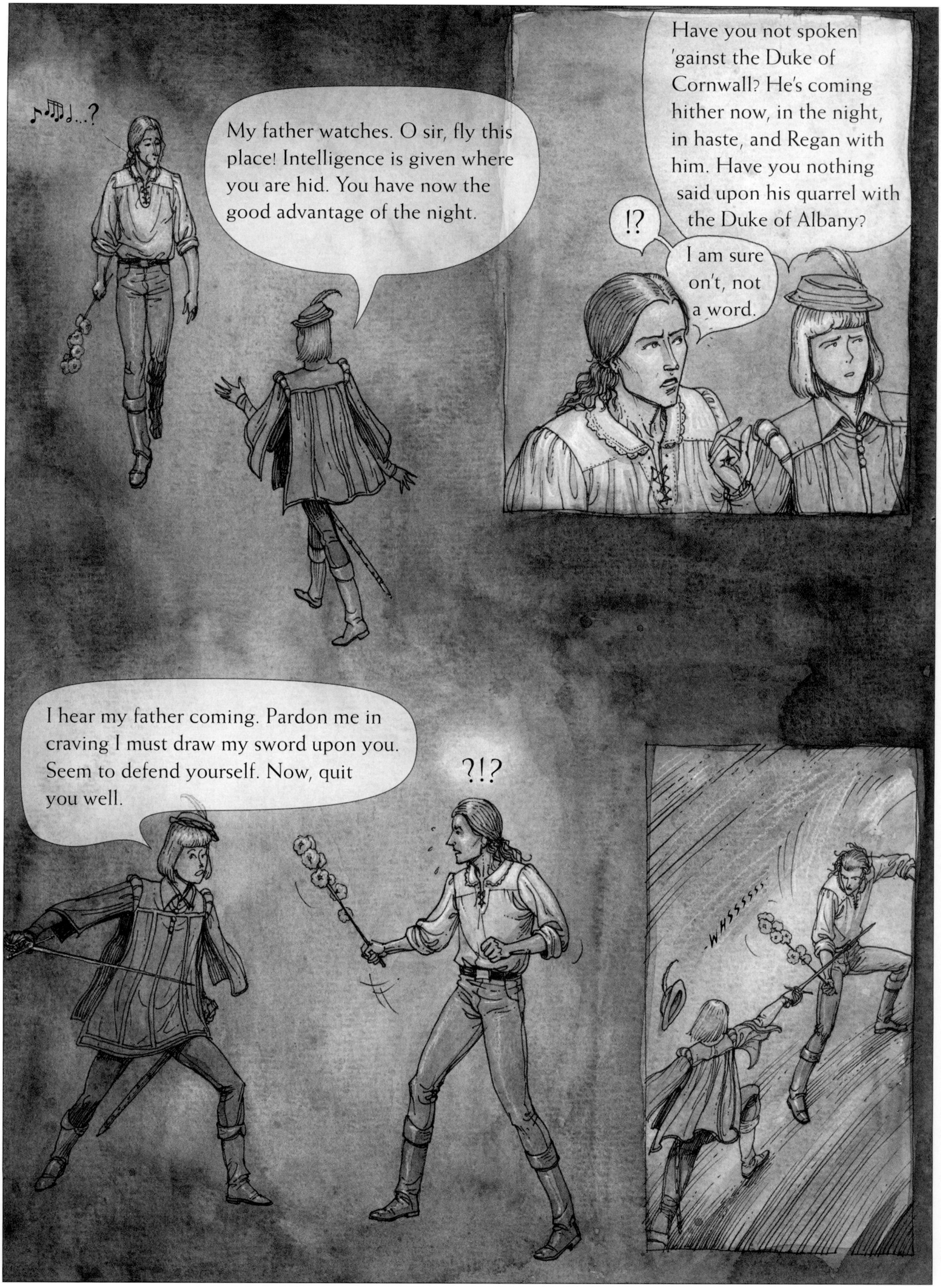
♪♫♩...?
My father watches. O sir, fly this place! Intelligence is given where you are hid. You have now the good advantage of the night.
Have you not spoken 'gainst the Duke of Cornwall? He's coming hither now, in the night, in haste, and Regan with him. Have you nothing said upon his quarrel with the Duke of Albany?
!?
I am sure on't, not a word.
I hear my father coming. Pardon me in craving I must draw my sword upon you. Seem to defend yourself. Now, quit you well.
?!?
-WHSSSSSS

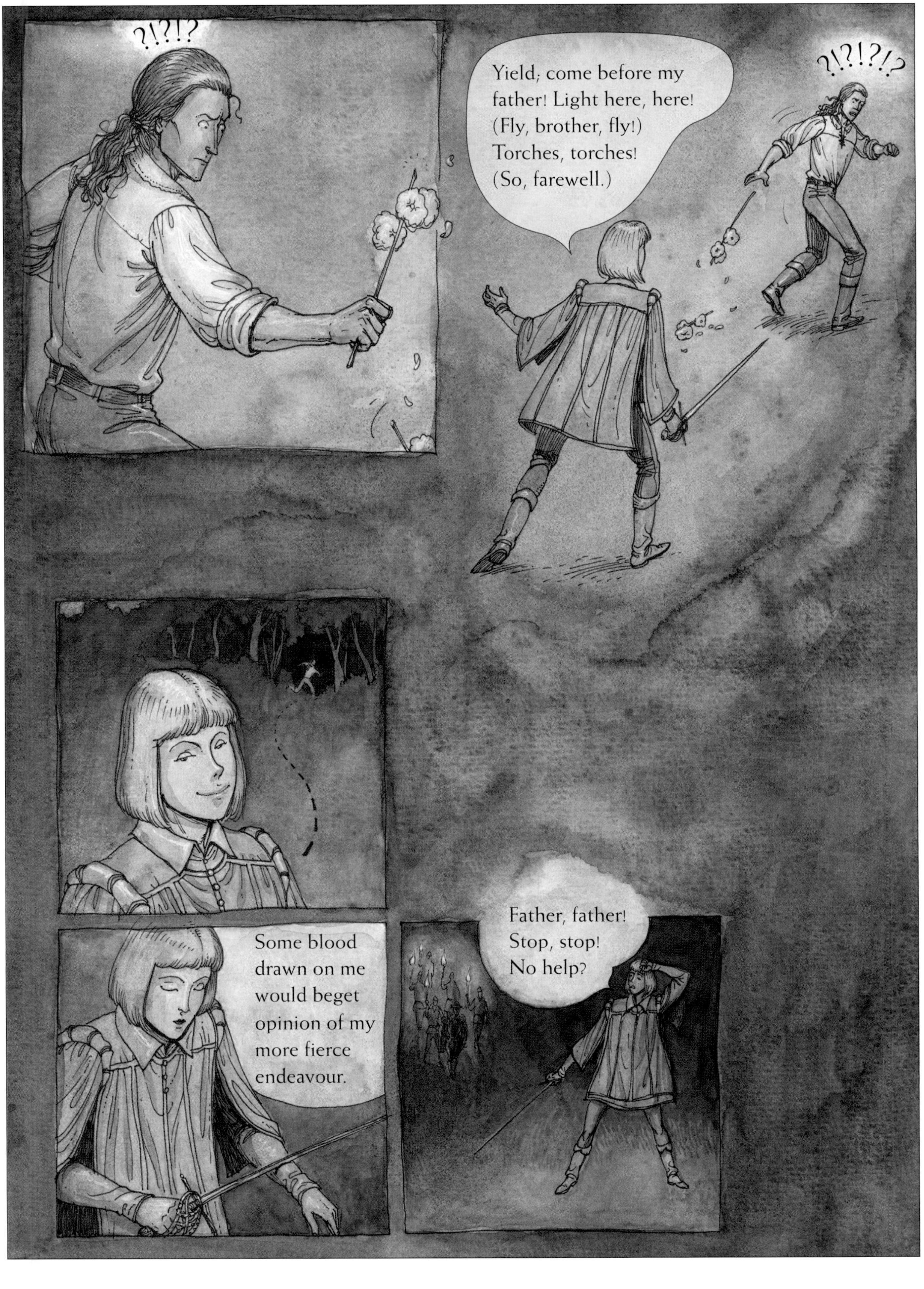
?!?!?
Yield; come before my father! Light here, here! (Fly, brother, fly!) Torches, torches! (So, farewell.)
?!?!?!?
Some blood drawn on me would beget opinion of my more fierce endeavour.
Father, father! Stop, stop! No help?

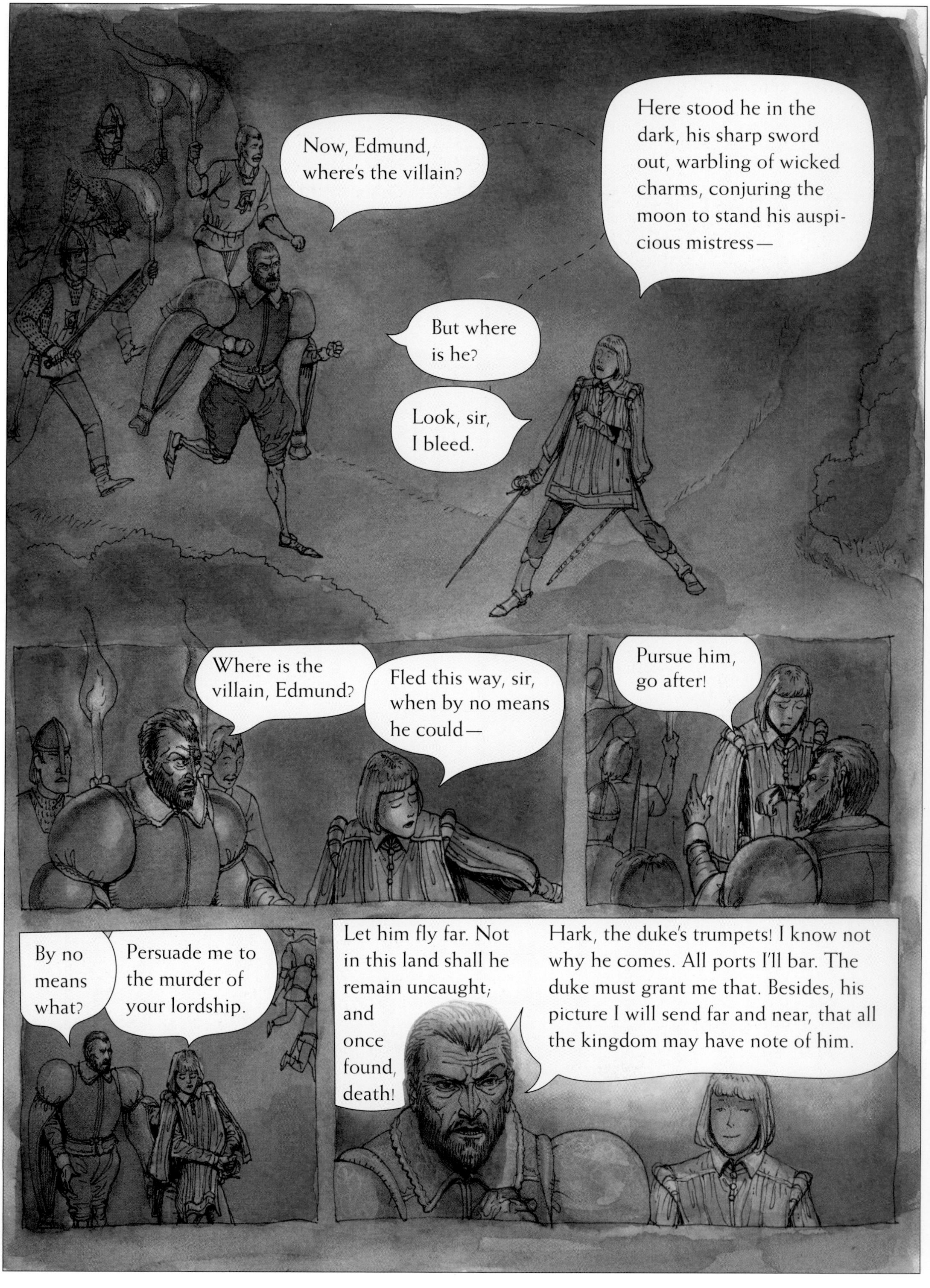
Now, Edmund, where's the villain?
Here stood he in the dark, his sharp sword out, warbling of wicked charms, conjuring the moon to stand his auspicious mistress—
But where is he?
Look, sir, I bleed.
Where is the villain, Edmund?
Fled this way, sir, when by no means he could—
Pursue him, go after!
By no means what?
Persuade me to the murder of your lordship.
Let him fly far. Not in this land shall he remain uncaught; and once found, death!
Hark, the duke's trumpets! I know not why he comes. All ports I'll bar. The duke must grant me that. Besides, his picture I will send far and near, that all the kingdom may have note of him.

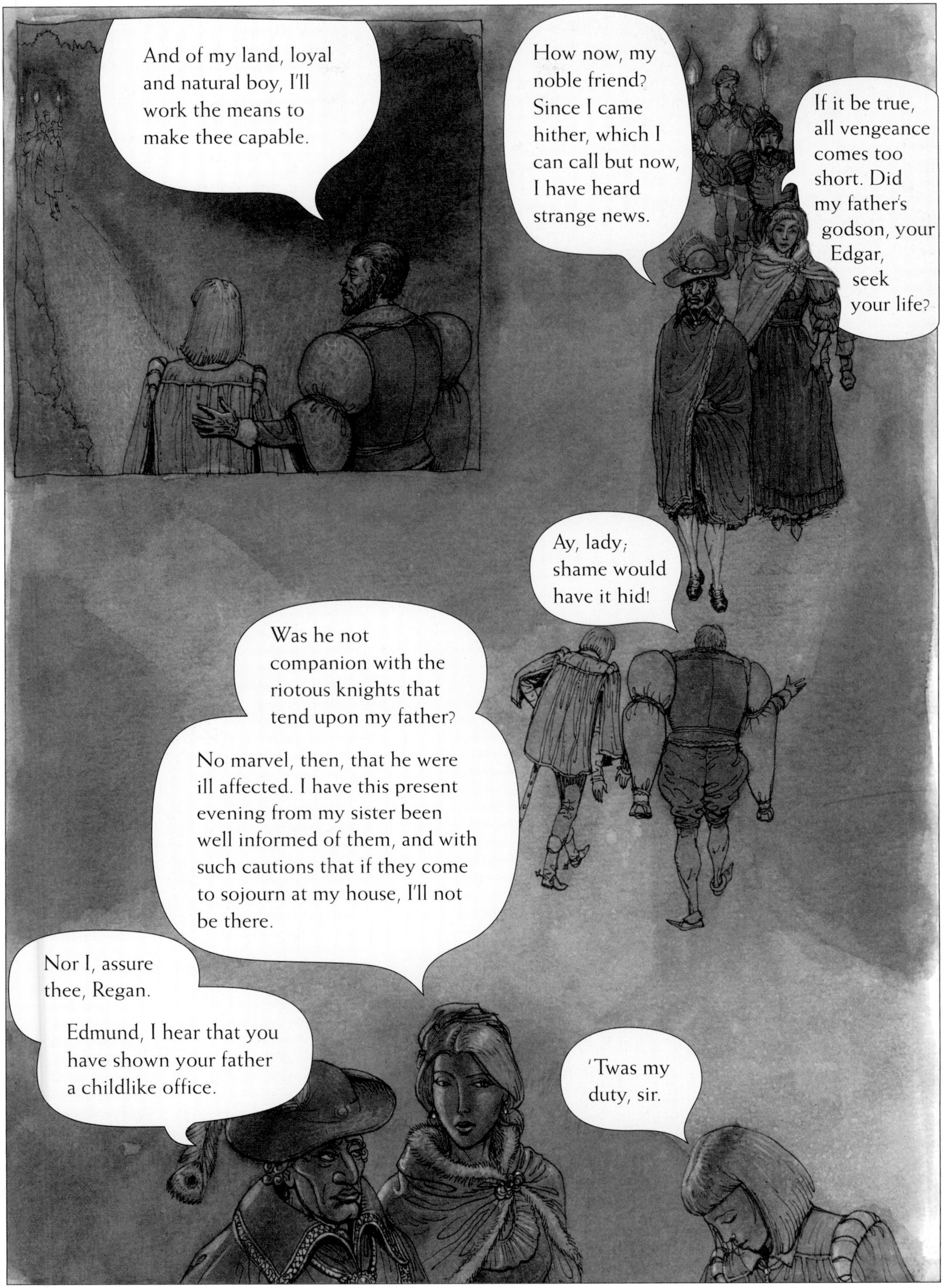
And of my land, loyal and natural boy, I'll work the means to make thee capable.
How now, my noble friend? Since I came hither, which I can call but now, I have heard strange news.
If it be true, all vengeance comes too short. Did my father's godson, your Edgar, seek your life?
Ay, lady; shame would have it hid!
Was he not companion with the riotous knights that tend upon my father?
No marvel, then, that he were ill affected. I have this present evening from my sister been well informed of them, and with such cautions that if they come to sojourn at my house, I'll not be there.
Nor I, assure thee, Regan.
Edmund, I hear that you have shown your father a childlike office.
'Twas my duty, sir.

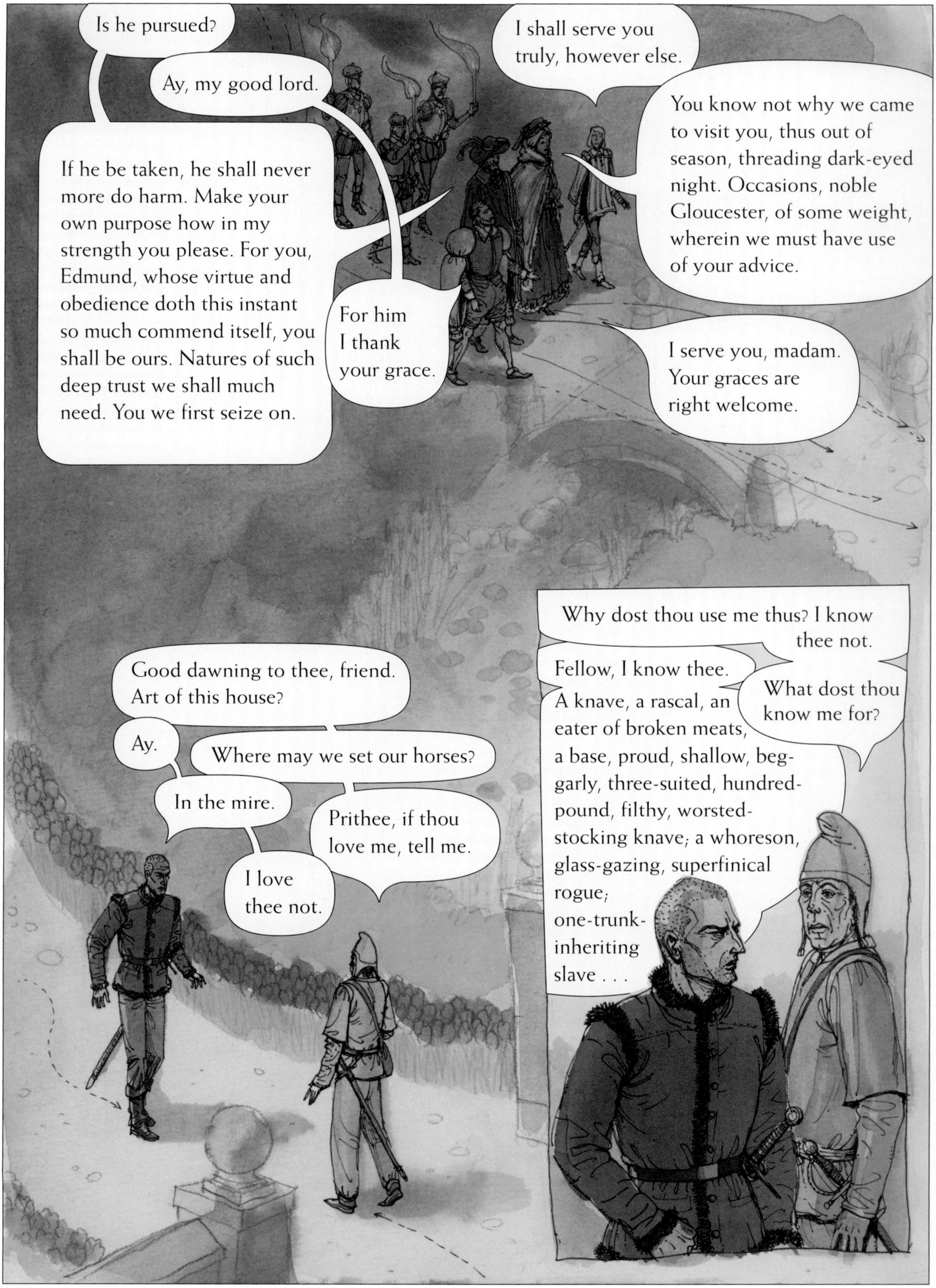
Is he pursued?
Ay, my good lord.
If he be taken, he shall never more do harm. Make your own purpose how in my strength you please. For you, Edmund, whose virtue and obedience doth this instant so much commend itself, you shall be ours. Natures of such deep trust we shall much need. You we first seize on.
For him I thank your grace.
I shall serve you truly, however else.
You know not why we came to visit you, thus out of season, threading dark-eyed night. Occasions, noble Gloucester, of some weight, wherein we must have use of your advice.
I serve you, madam. Your graces are right welcome.
Good dawning to thee, friend. Art of this house?
Ay.
Where may we set our horses?
In the mire.
Prithee, if thou love me, tell me.
I love thee not.
Why dost thou use me thus? I know thee not.
Fellow, I know thee.
What dost thou know me for?
A knave, a rascal, an eater of broken meats, a base, proud, shallow, beggarly, three-suited, hundred-pound, filthy, worsted-stocking knave; a whoreson, glass-gazing, superfinical rogue; one-trunk-inheriting slave . . .

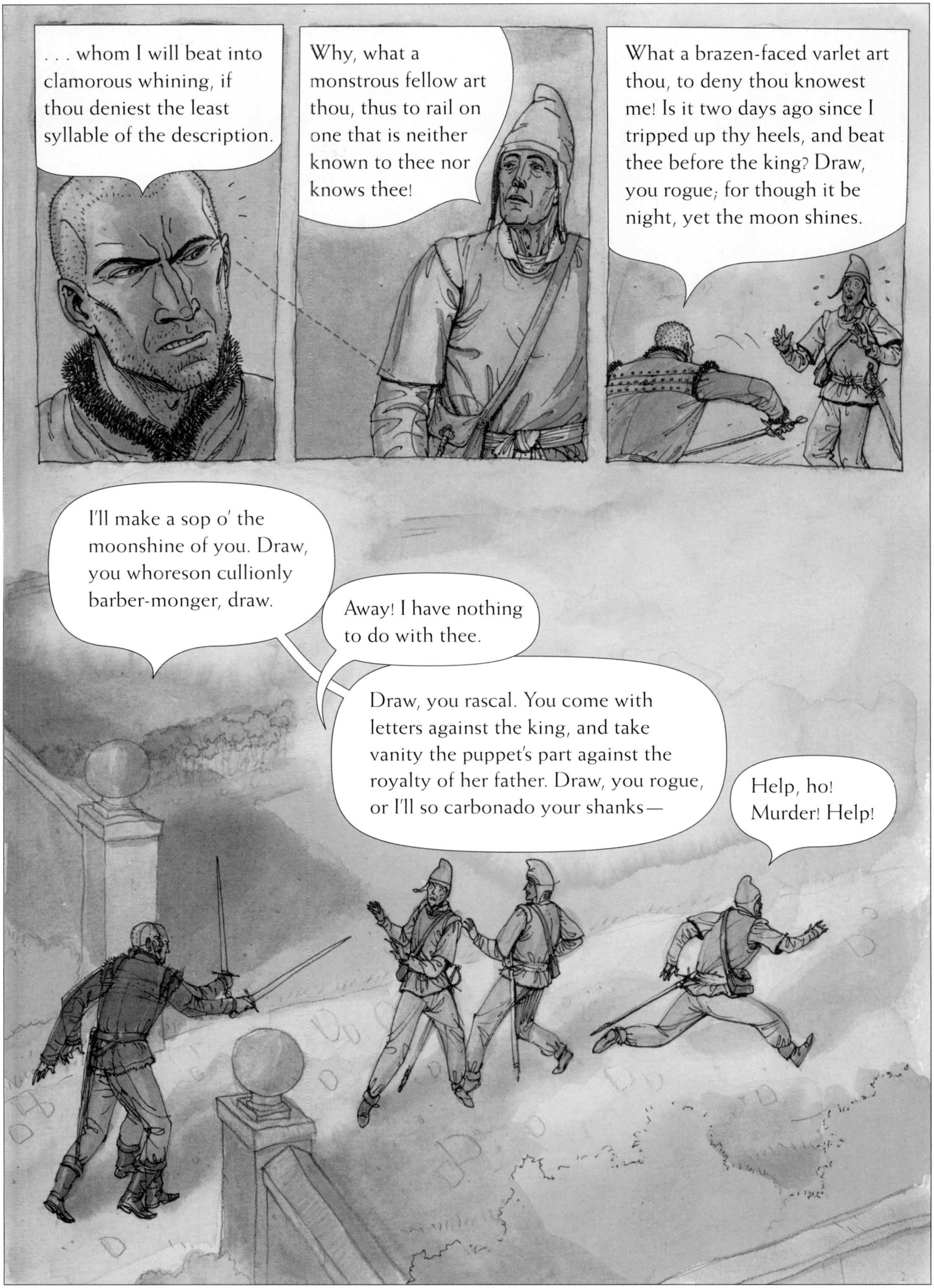
. . . whom I will beat into clamorous whining, if thou deniest the least syllable of the description.
Why, what a monstrous fellow art thou, thus to rail on one that is neither known to thee nor knows thee!
What a brazen-faced varlet art thou, to deny thou knowest me! Is it two days ago since I tripped up thy heels, and beat thee before the king? Draw, you rogue; for though it be night, yet the moon shines.
I'll make a sop o' the moonshine of you. Draw, you whoreson cullionly barber-monger, draw.
Away! I have nothing to do with thee.
Draw, you rascal. You come with letters against the king, and take vanity the puppet's part against the royalty of her father. Draw, you rogue, or I'll so carbonado your shanks—
Help, ho! Murder! Help!

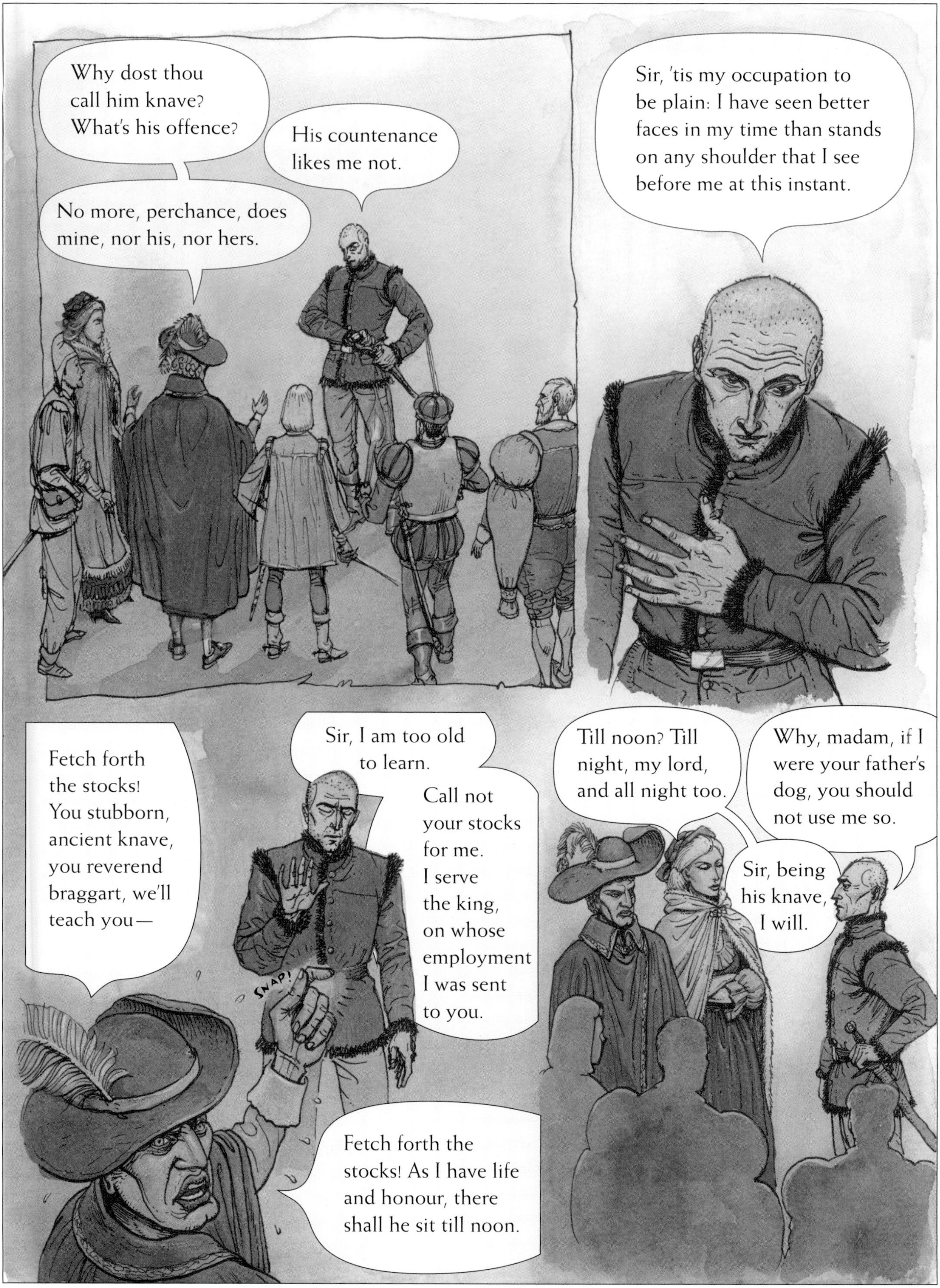
Why dost thou call him knave? What's his offence?
His countenance likes me not.
No more, perchance, does mine, nor his, nor hers.
Sir, 'tis my occupation to be plain: I have seen better faces in my time than stands on any shoulder that I see before me at this instant.
Fetch forth the stocks! You stubborn, ancient knave, you reverend braggart, we'll teach you—
Sir, I am too old to learn.
Call not your stocks for me. I serve the king, on whose employment I was sent to you.
SNAP!
Fetch forth the stocks! As I have life and honour, there shall he sit till noon.
Till noon? Till night, my lord, and all night too.
Why, madam, if I were your father's dog, you should not use me so.
Sir, being his knave, I will.

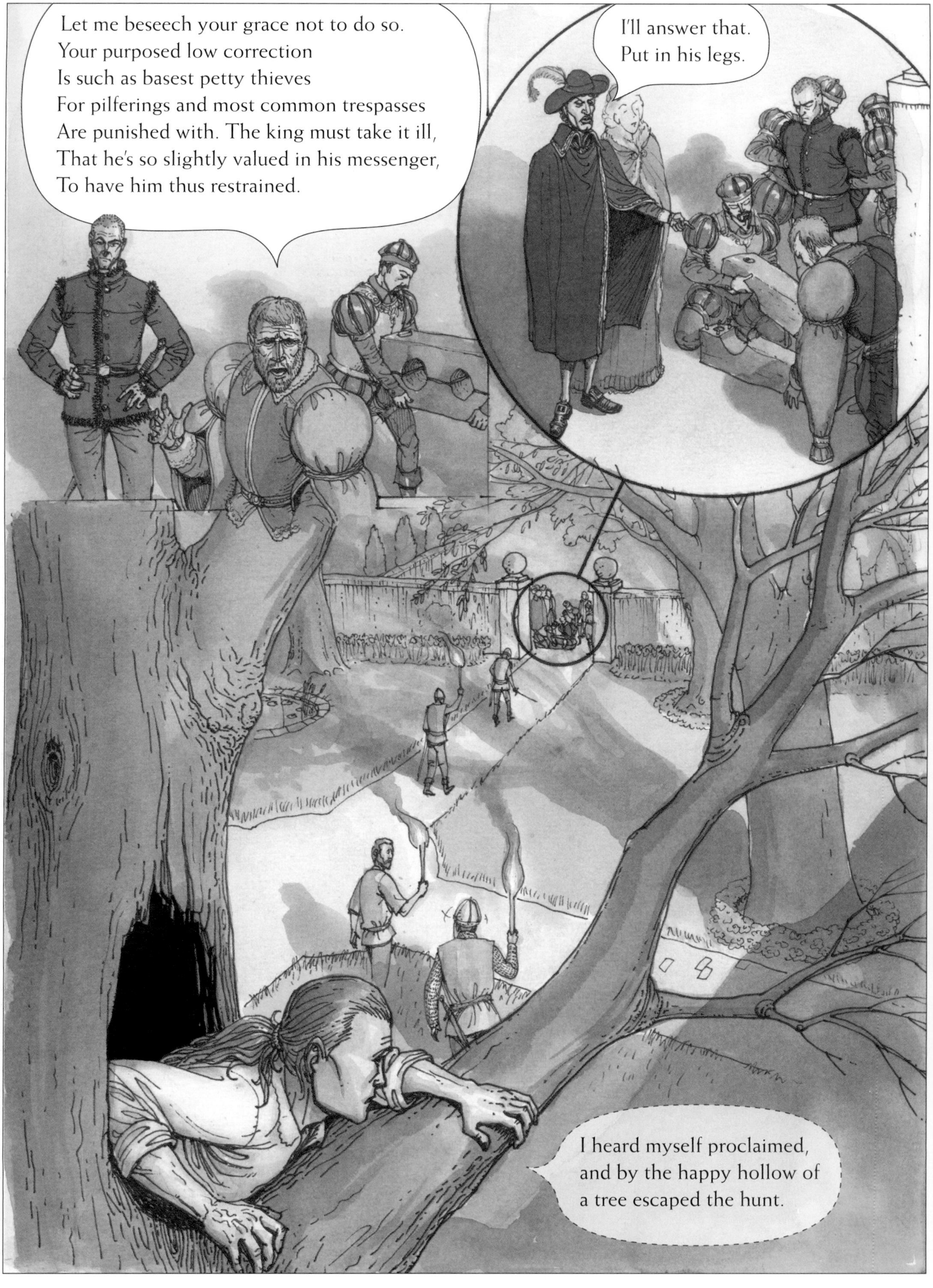
Let me beseech your grace not to do so.
Your purposed low correction
Is such as basest petty thieves
For pilferings and most common trespasses
Are punished with. The king must take it ill,
That he's so slightly valued in his messenger,
To have him thus restrained.
I'll answer that.
Put in his legs.
I heard myself proclaimed,
and by the happy hollow of
a tree escaped the hunt.

No port is free, no place
That guard and most unusual vigilance
Does not attend my capture.

Whiles I may 'scape
I will preserve myself, and am bethought
To take the basest and most poorest shape
That ever penury, in contempt of man,
Brought near to beast.

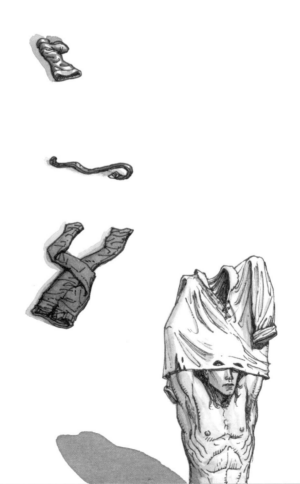

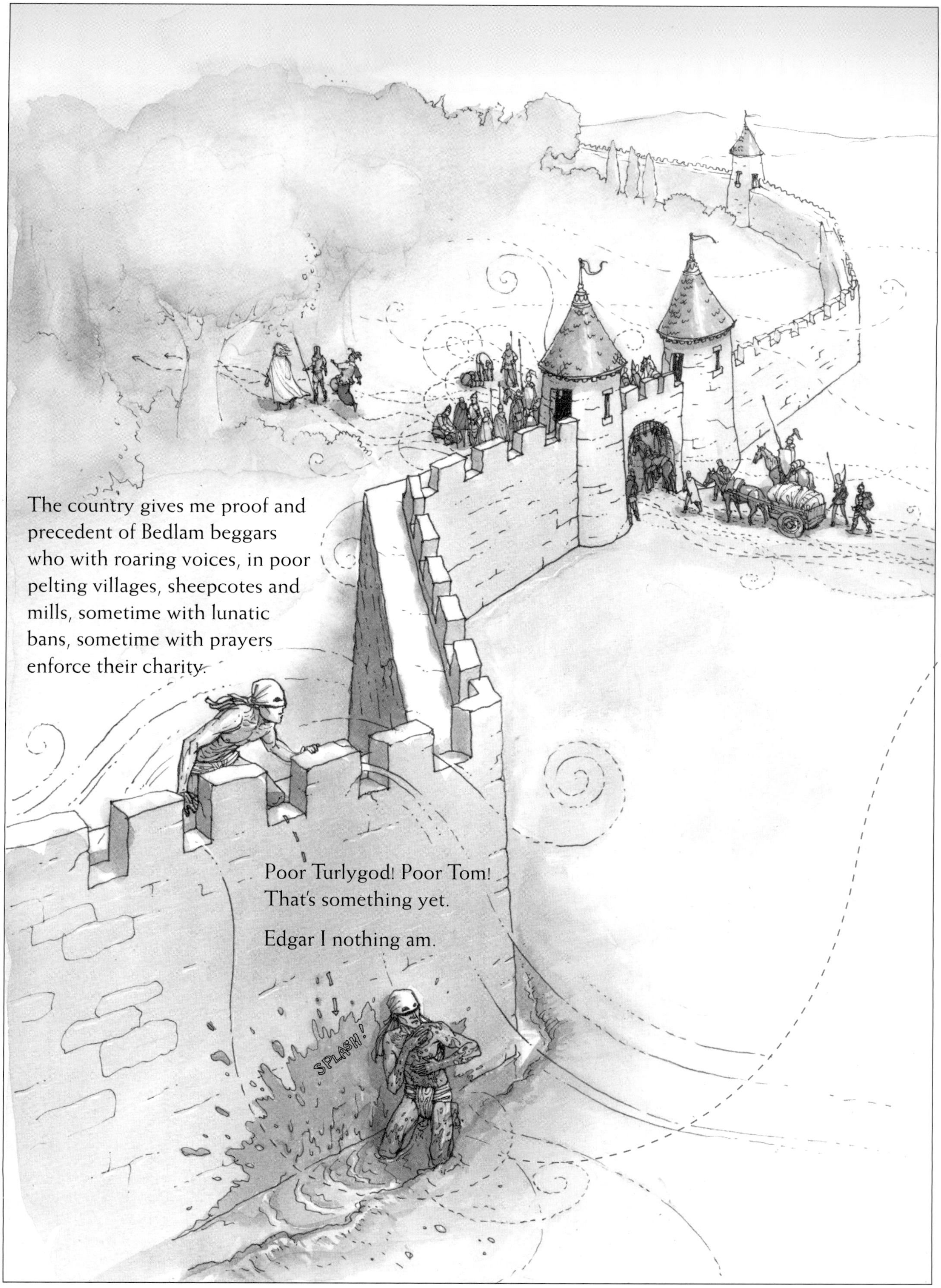
The country gives me proof and precedent of Bedlam beggars who with roaring voices, in poor pelting villages, sheepcotes and mills, sometime with lunatic bans, sometime with prayers enforce their charity.
Poor Turlygod! Poor Tom! That's something yet.
Edgar I nothing am.
SPLASH!

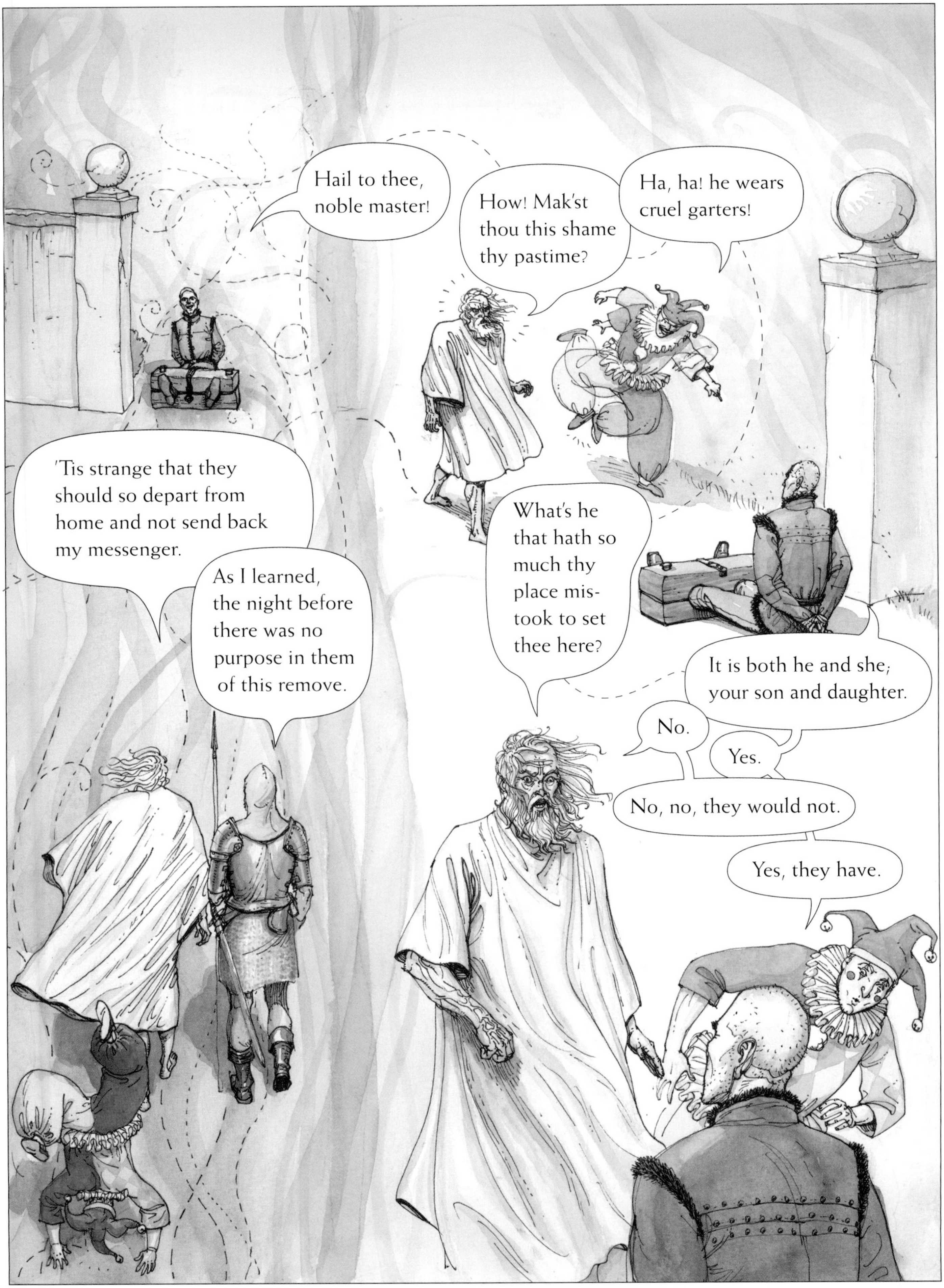
Hail to thee, noble master!
How! Mak'st thou this shame thy pastime?
Ha, ha! he wears cruel garters!
'Tis strange that they should so depart from home and not send back my messenger.
As I learned, the night before there was no purpose in them of this remove.
What's he that hath so much thy place mis-took to set thee here?
It is both he and she; your son and daughter.
No.
Yes.
No, no, they would not.
Yes, they have.

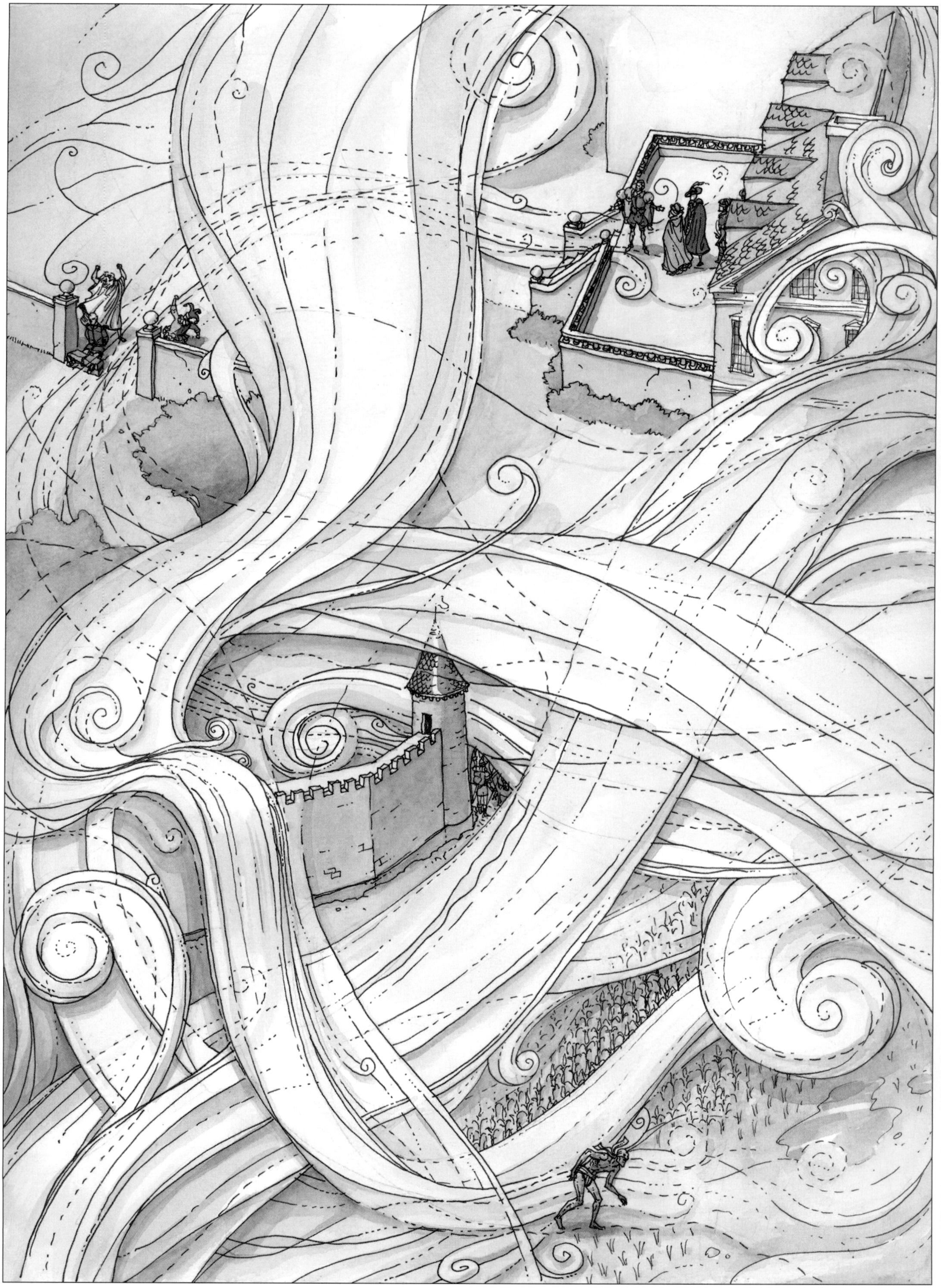

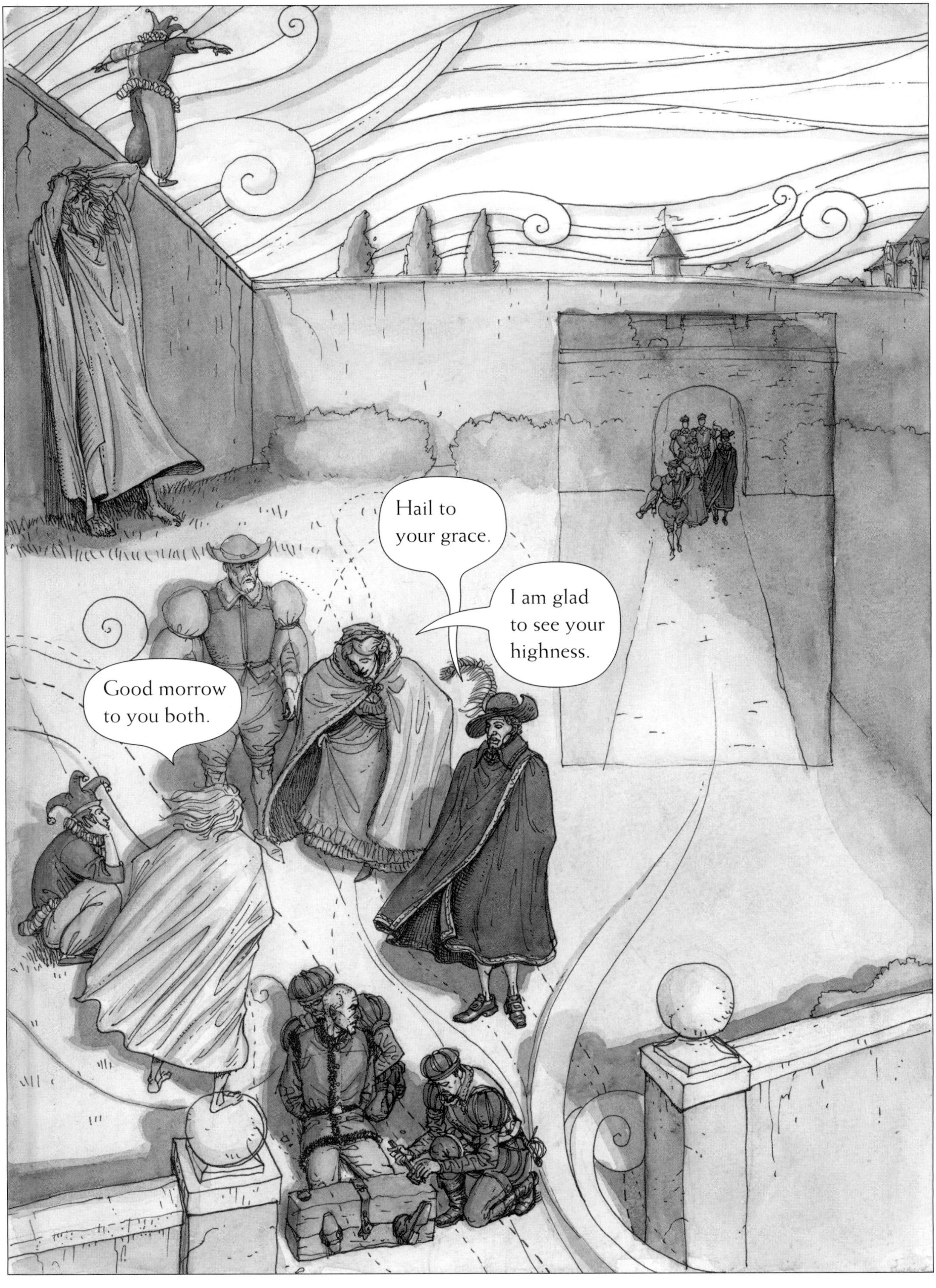
Hail to your grace.
I am glad to see your highness.
Good morrow to you both.

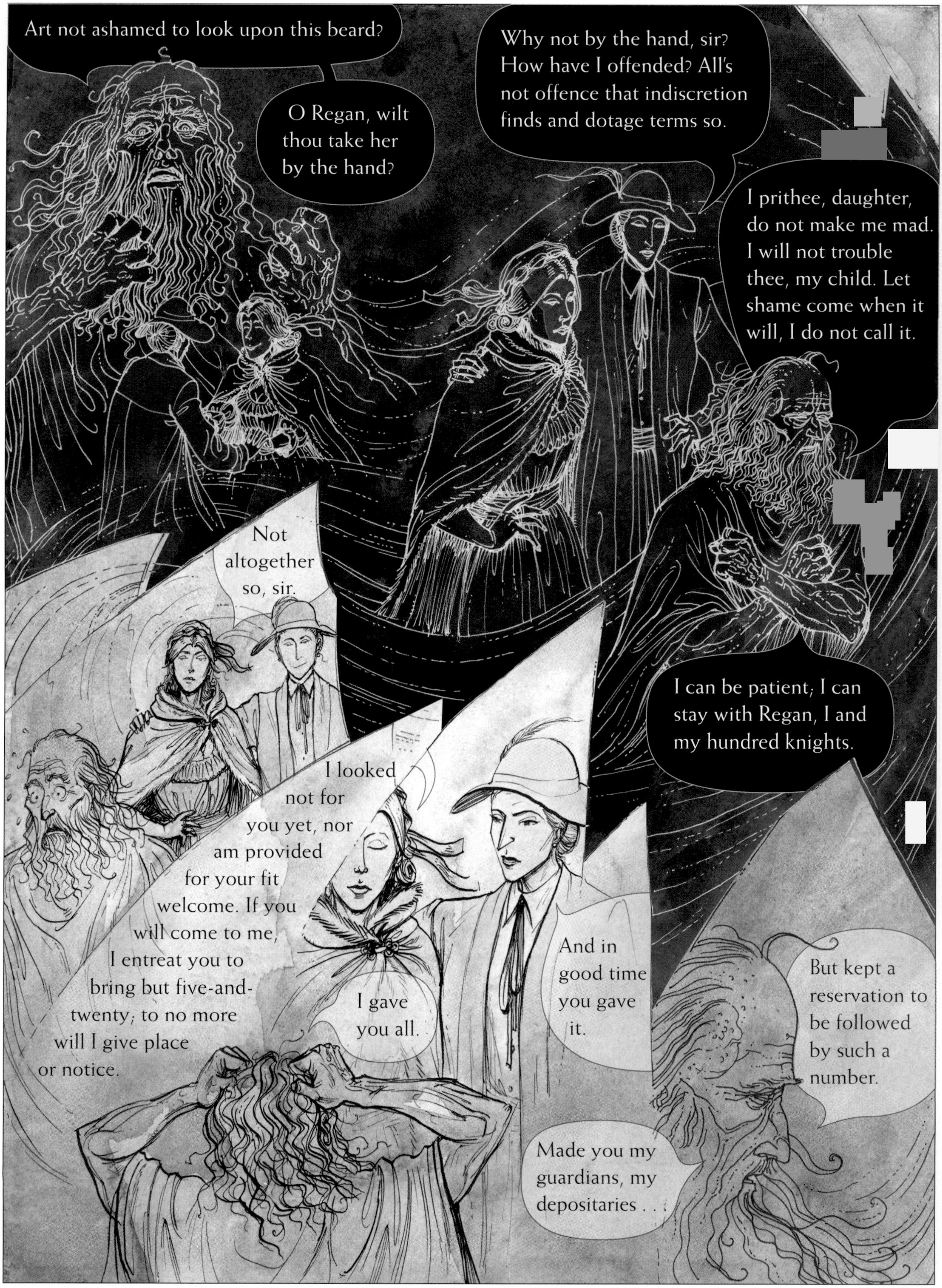
Art not ashamed to look upon this beard?
O Regan, wilt thou take her by the hand?
Why not by the hand, sir? How have I offended? All's not offence that indiscretion finds and dotage terms so.
I prithee, daughter, do not make me mad. I will not trouble thee, my child. Let shame come when it will, I do not call it.
I can be patient; I can stay with Regan, I and my hundred knights.
Not altogether so, sir.
I looked not for you yet, nor am provided for your fit welcome. If you will come to me, I entreat you to bring but five-and-twenty; to no more will I give place or notice.
I gave you all.
And in good time you gave it.
But kept a reservation to be followed by such a number.
Made you my guardians, my depositaries . . .

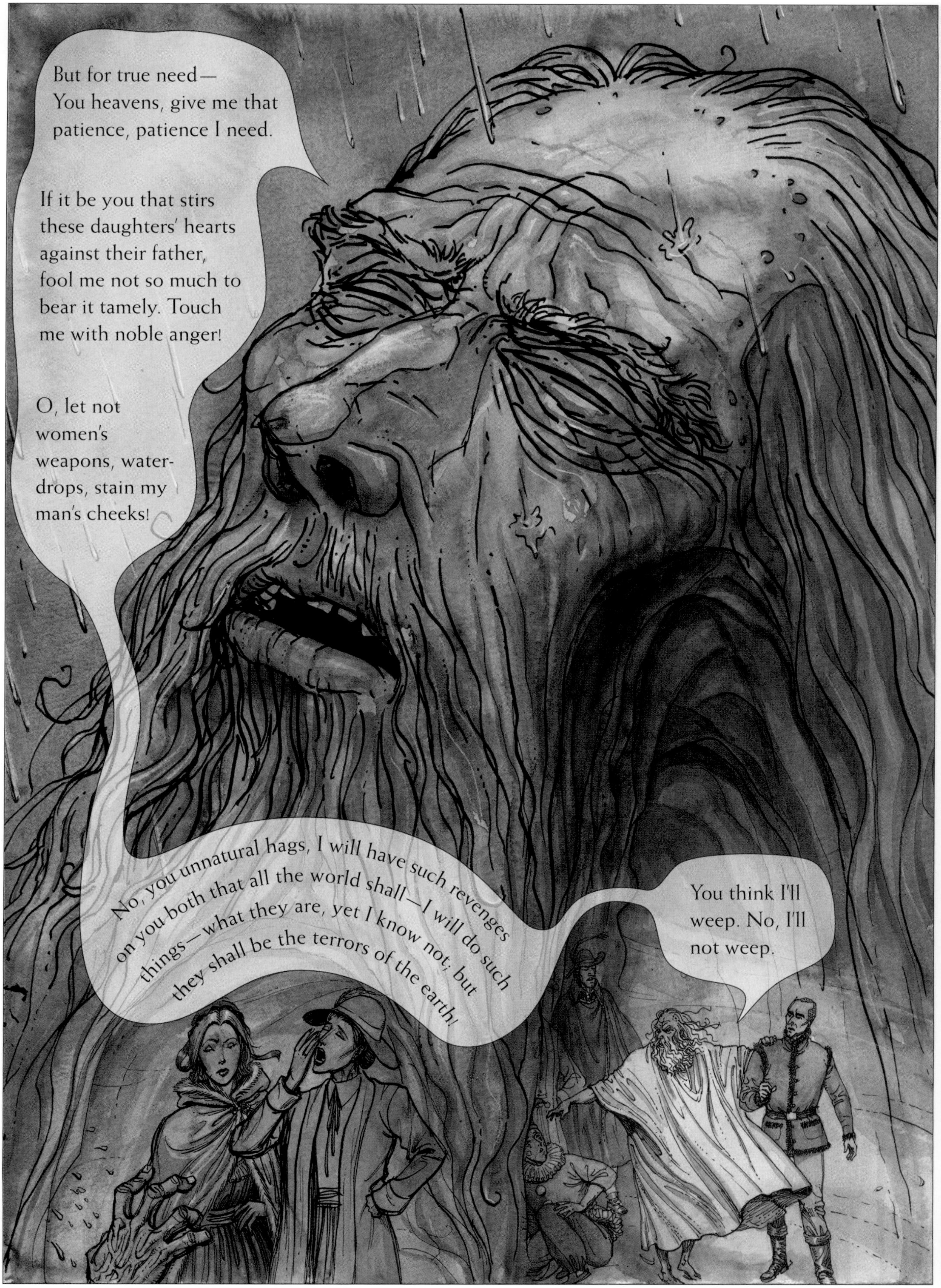
But for true need— You heavens, give me that patience, patience I need.
If it be you that stirs these daughters' hearts against their father, fool me not so much to bear it tamely. Touch me with noble anger!
O, let not women's weapons, water-drops, stain my man's cheeks!
No, you unnatural hags, I will have such revenges on you both that all the world shall—I will do such things—what they are, yet I know not; but they shall be the terrors of the earth!
You think I'll weep. No, I'll not weep.

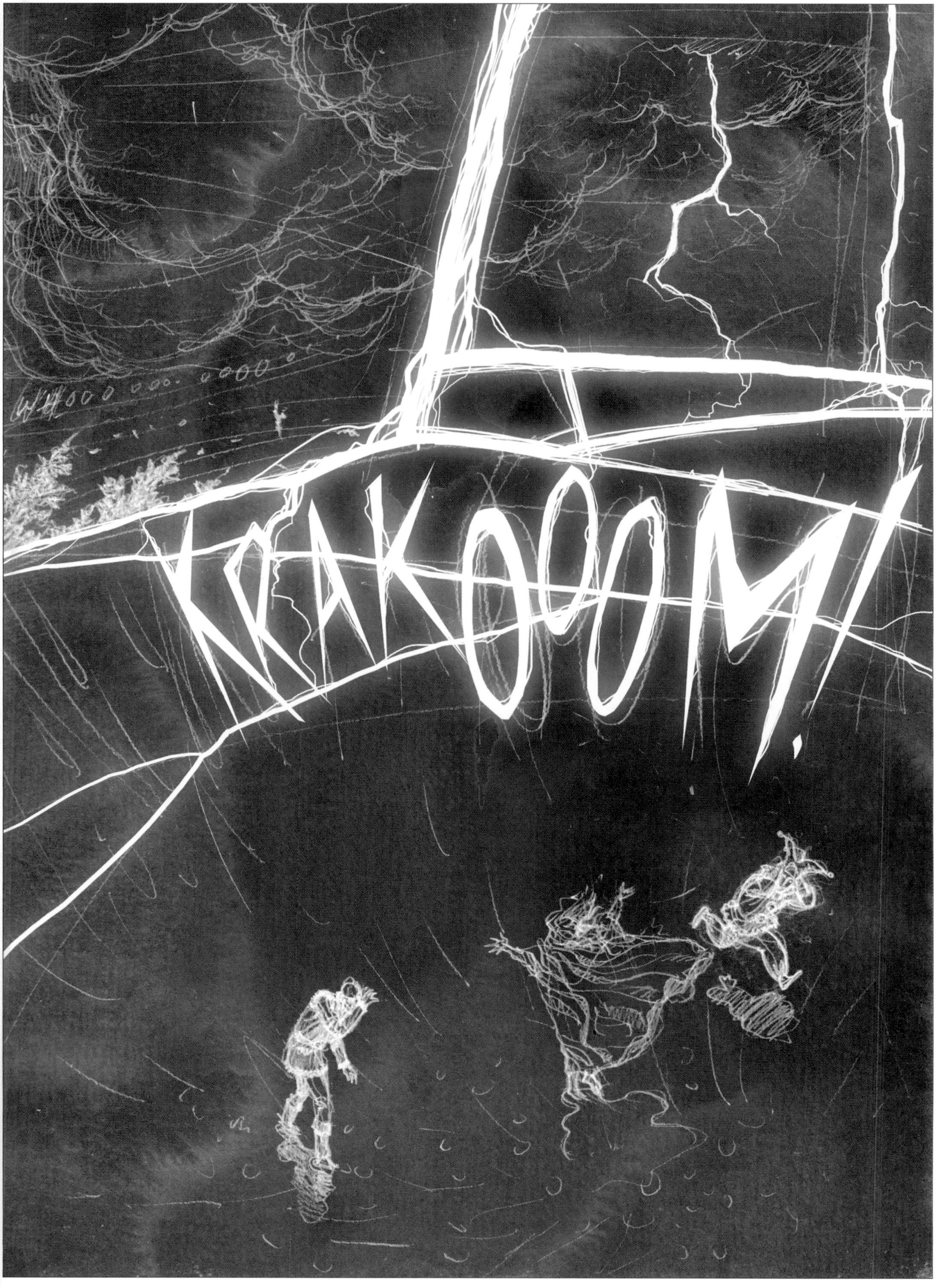
WHOOOO OOO. OOOOO
KRAKOOOM!

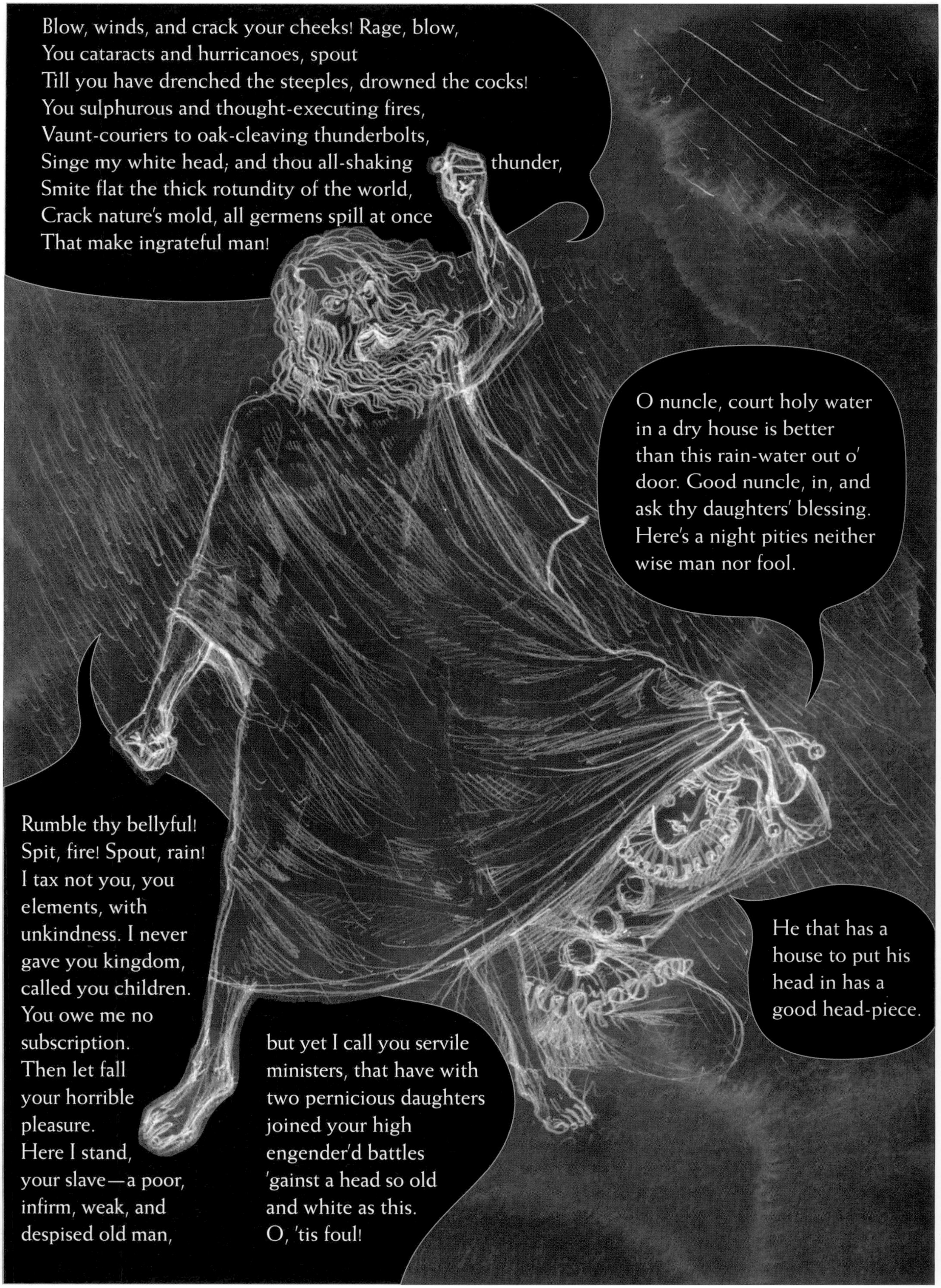
Blow, winds, and crack your cheeks! Rage, blow, You cataracts and hurricanoes, spout Till you have drenched the steeples, drowned the cocks! You sulphurous and thought-executing fires, Vaunt-couriers to oak-cleaving thunderbolts, Singe my white head; and thou all-shaking thunder, Smite flat the thick rotundity of the world, Crack nature's mold, all germens spill at once That make ingrateful man!
O nuncle, court holy water in a dry house is better than this rain-water out o' door. Good nuncle, in, and ask thy daughters' blessing. Here's a night pities neither wise man nor fool.
Rumble thy bellyful! Spit, fire! Spout, rain! I tax not you, you elements, with unkindness. I never gave you kingdom, called you children. You owe me no subscription. Then let fall your horrible pleasure. Here I stand, your slave—a poor, infirm, weak, and despised old man,
but yet I call you servile ministers, that have with two pernicious daughters joined your high engender'd battles 'gainst a head so old and white as this. O, 'tis foul!
He that has a house to put his head in has a good head-piece.

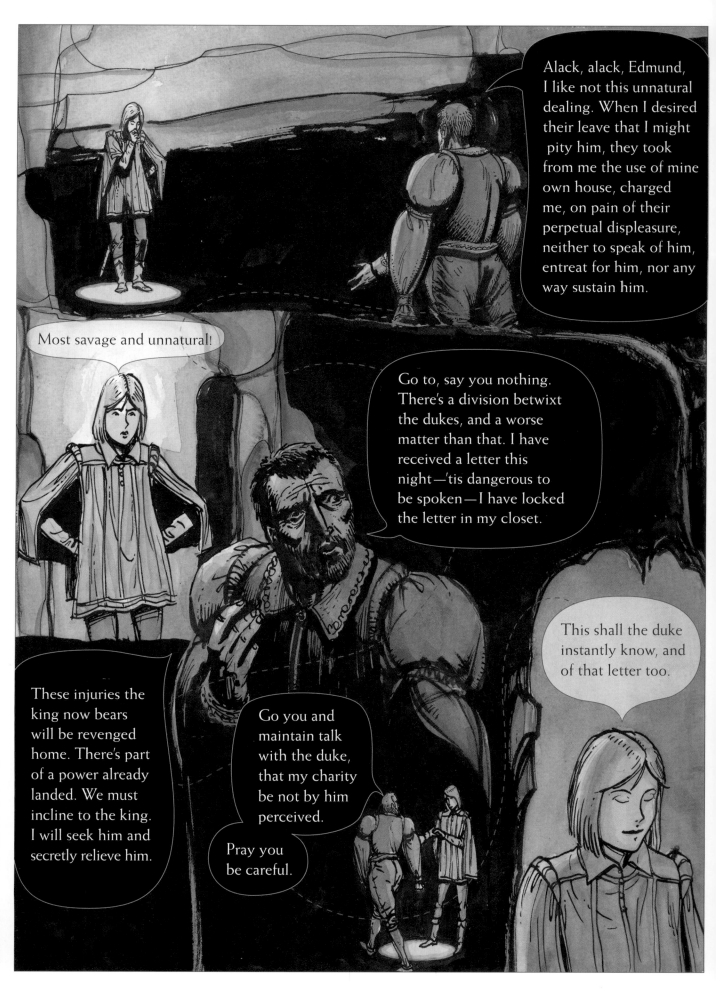

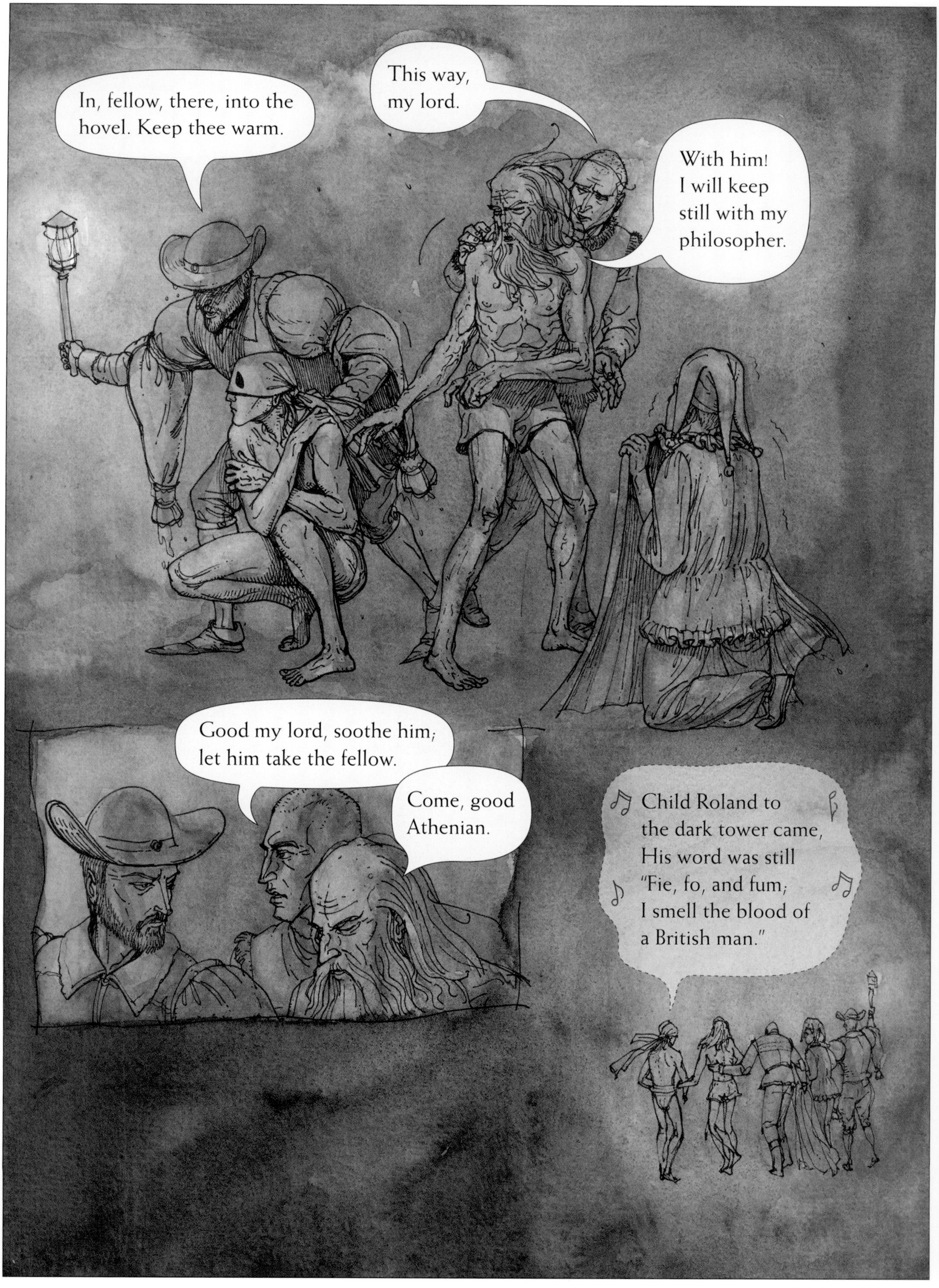
In, fellow, there, into the hovel. Keep thee warm.
This way, my lord.
With him! I will keep still with my philosopher.
Good my lord, soothe him; let him take the fellow.
Come, good Athenian.
Child Roland to the dark tower came, His word was still "Fie, fo, and fum; I smell the blood of a British man."

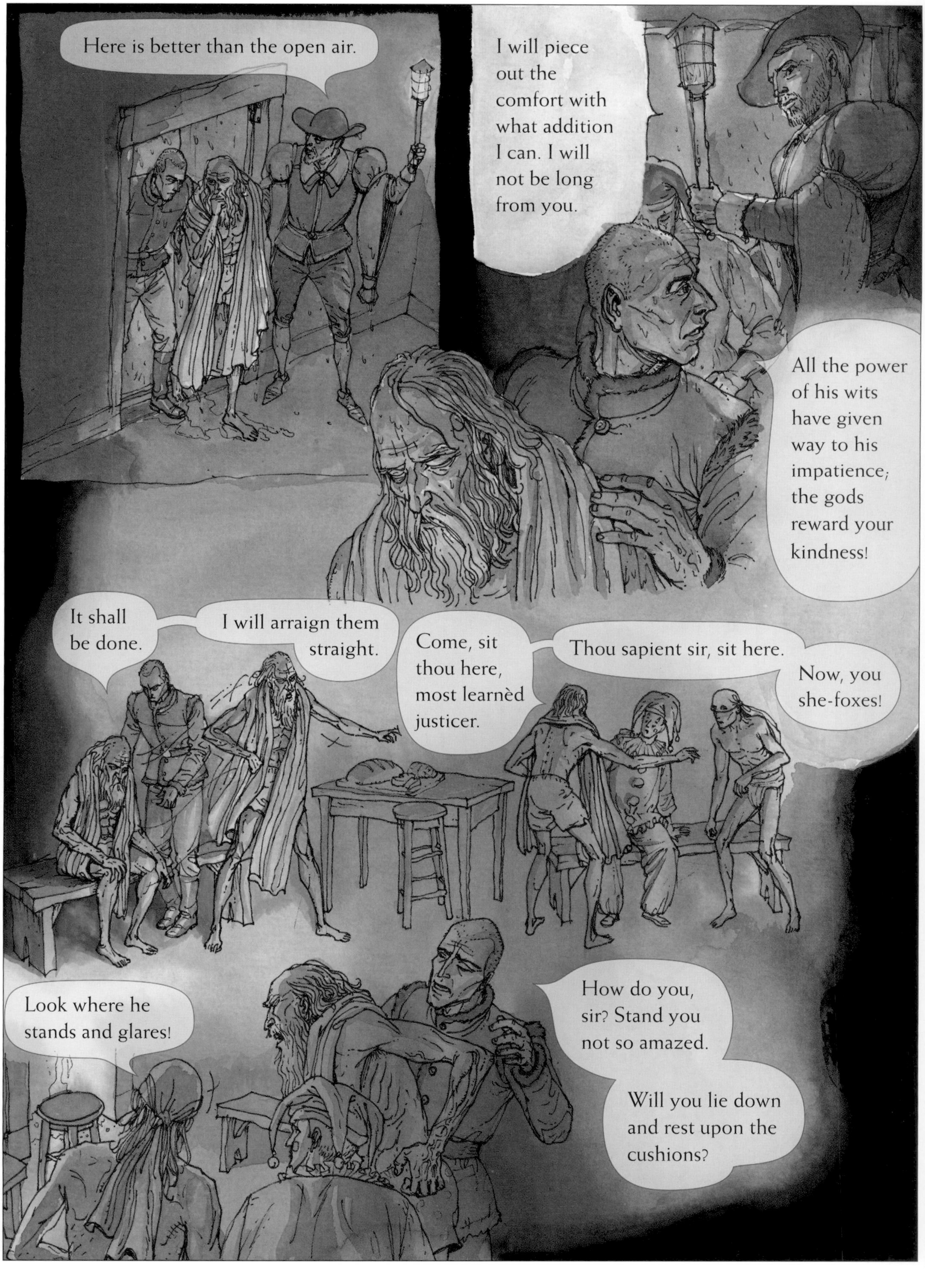
Here is better than the open air.
I will piece out the comfort with what addition I can. I will not be long from you.
All the power of his wits have given way to his impatience; the gods reward your kindness!
It shall be done.
I will arraign them straight.
Come, sit thou here, most learnèd justicer.
Thou sapient sir, sit here.
Now, you she-foxes!
Look where he stands and glares!
How do you, sir? Stand you not so amazed.
Will you lie down and rest upon the cushions?

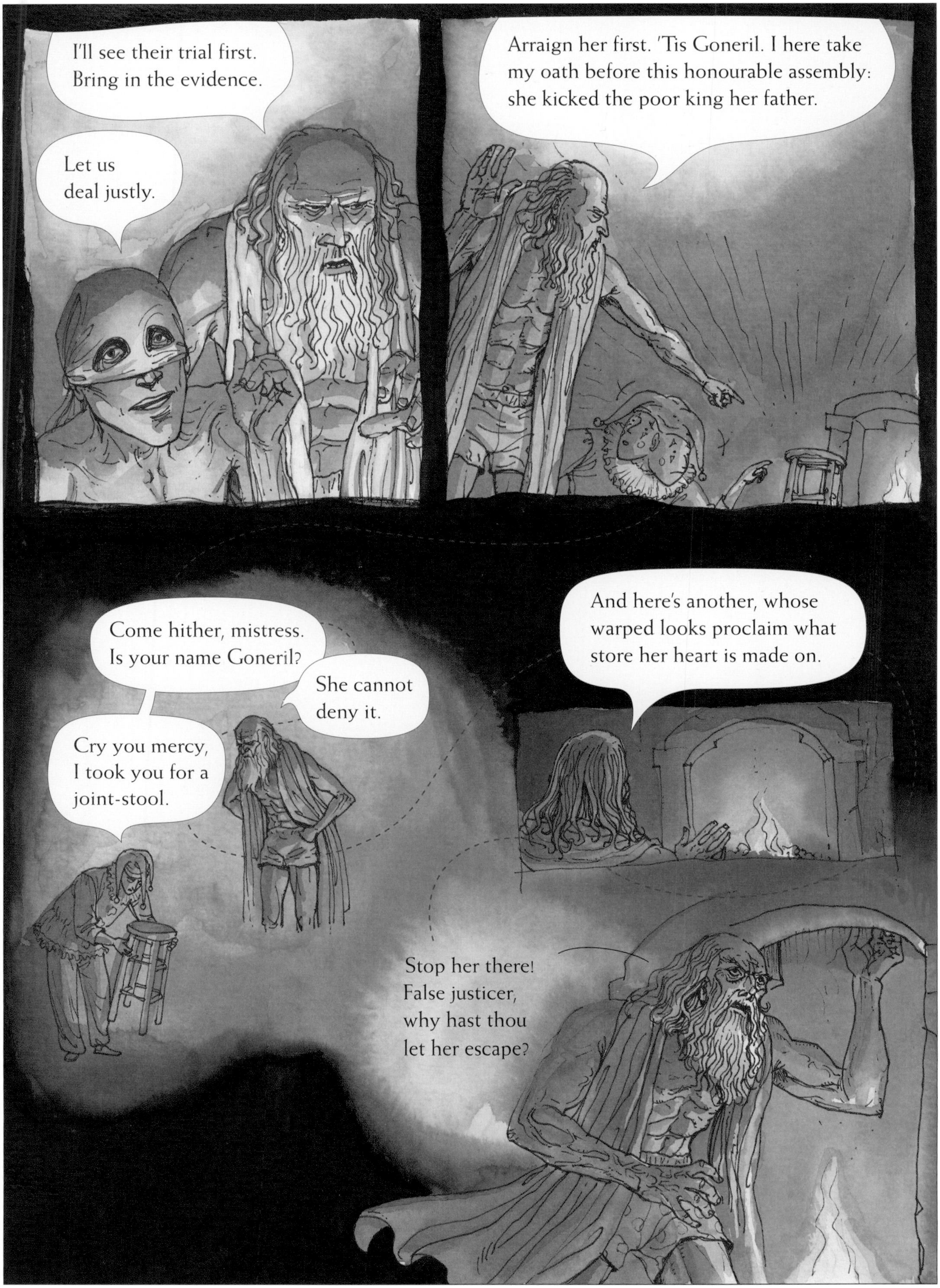
I'll see their trial first. Bring in the evidence.
Let us deal justly.
Arraign her first. 'Tis Goneril. I here take my oath before this honourable assembly: she kicked the poor king her father.
Come hither, mistress. Is your name Goneril?
She cannot deny it.
Cry you mercy, I took you for a joint-stool.
And here's another, whose warped looks proclaim what store her heart is made on.
Stop her there! False justicer, why hast thou let her escape?

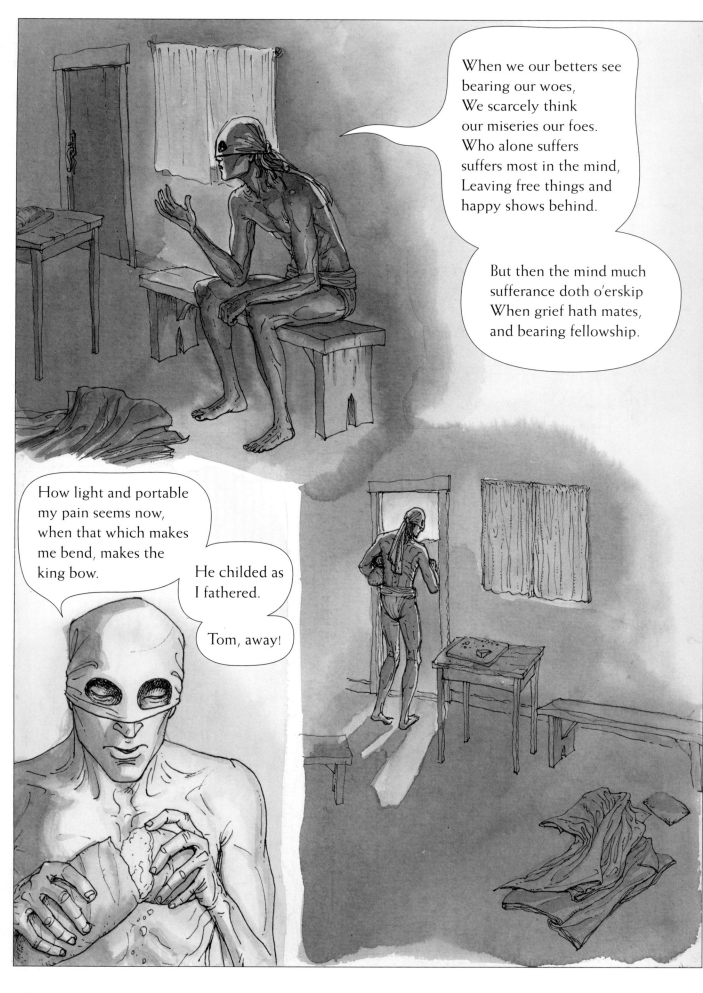

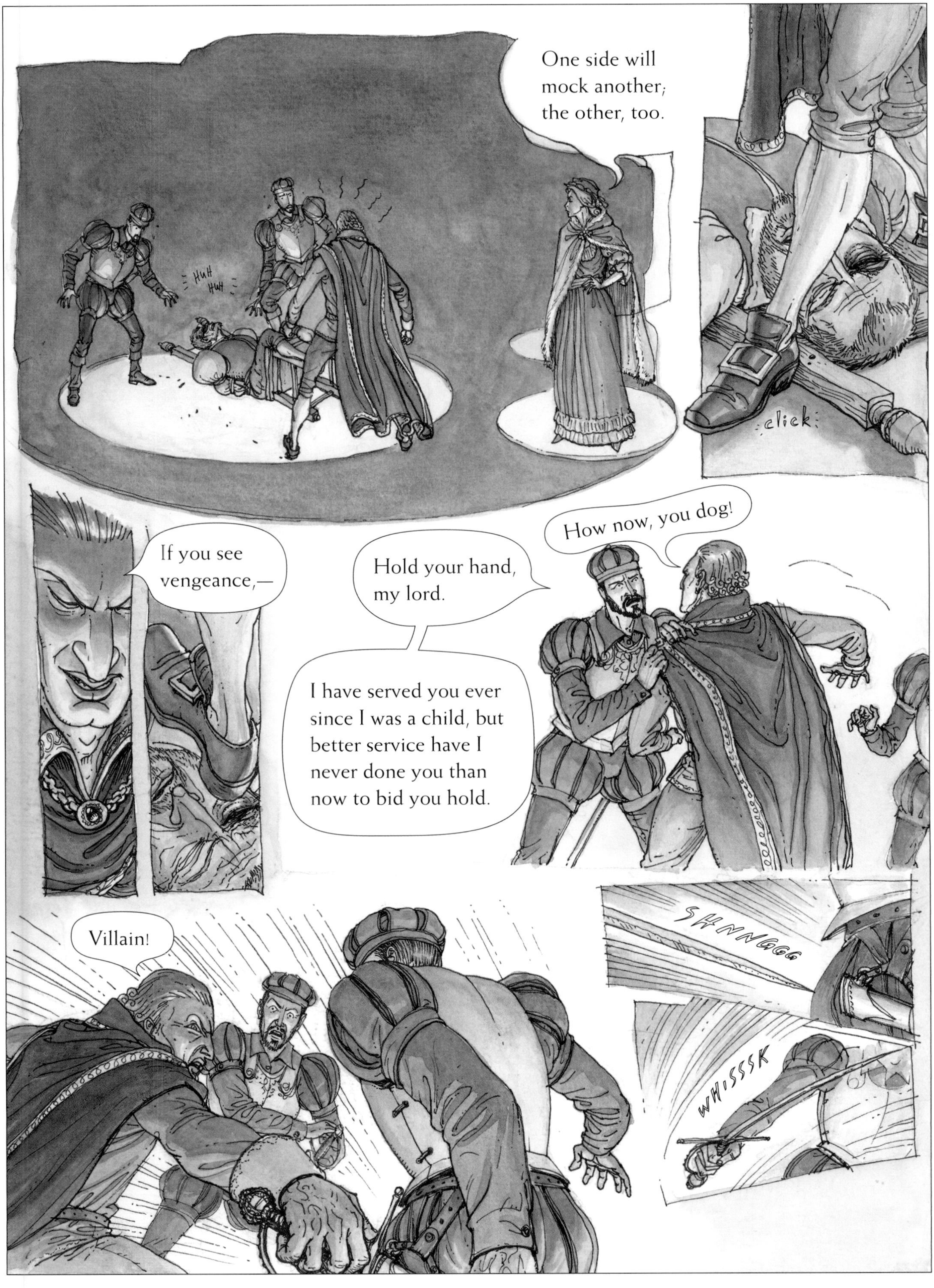

One side will mock another; the other, too.
HUH HUH
click
If you see vengeance,—
Hold your hand, my lord.
I have served you ever since I was a child, but better service have I never done you than now to bid you hold.
How now, you dog!
Villain!
SHNNGGG
WHISSSK

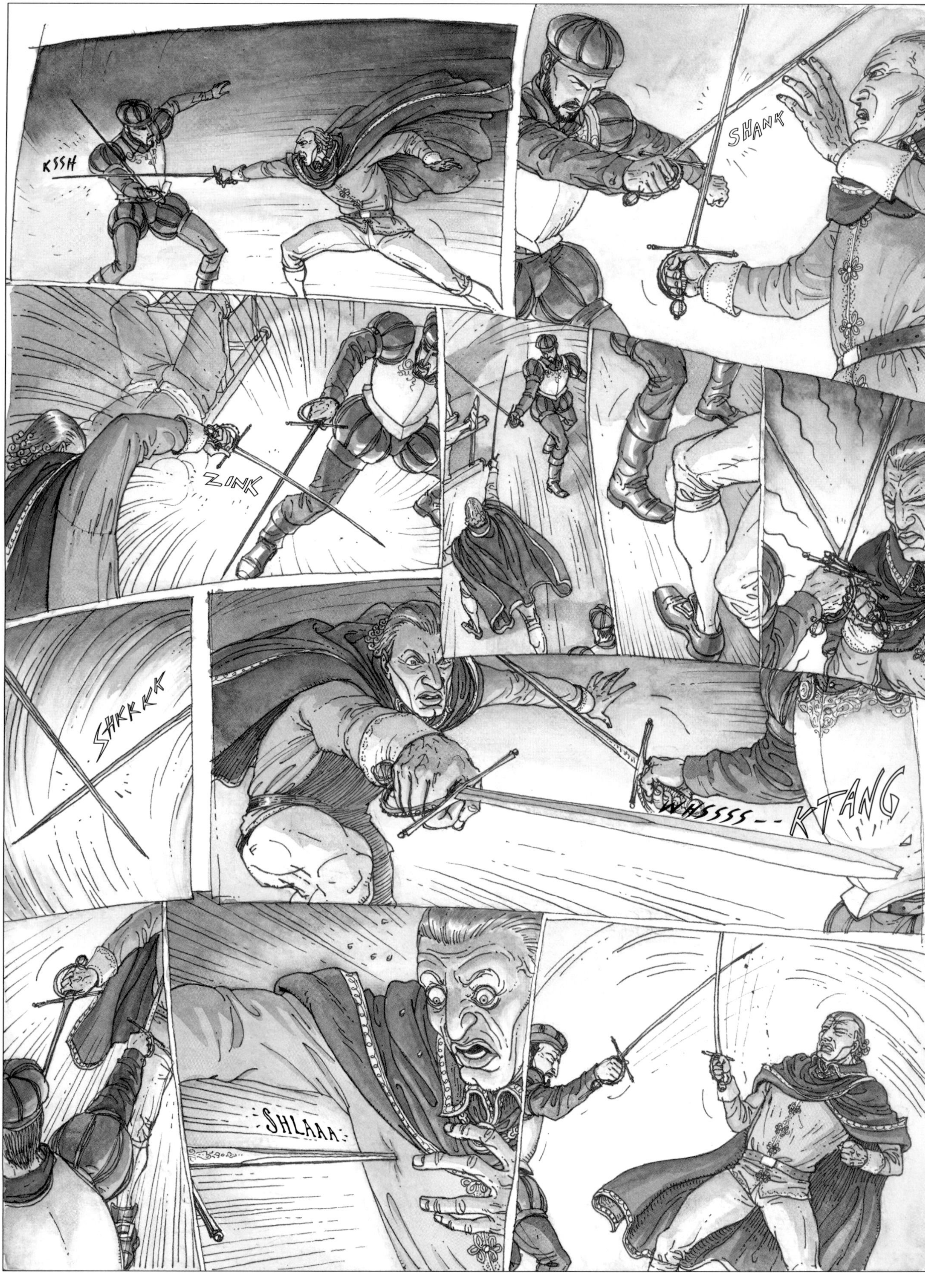
KSSH
SHANK
ZINK
SHKKKK
WHSSSS-- KTANG
SHLAAA

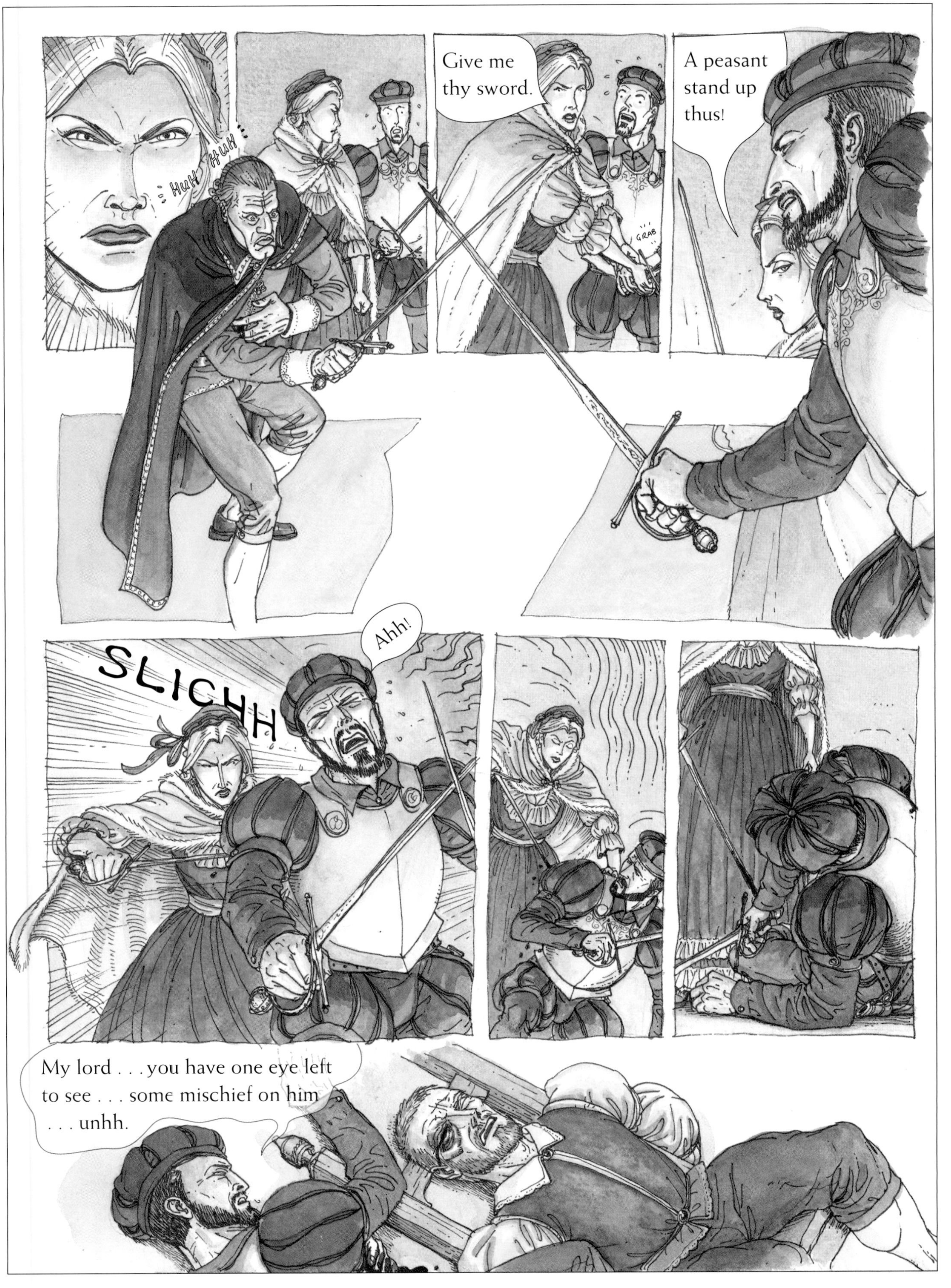
HUH HUH
Give me thy sword.
GRAB
A peasant stand up thus!
SLICHH
Ahh!
. . .
My lord . . . you have one eye left to see . . . some mischief on him . . . unhh.

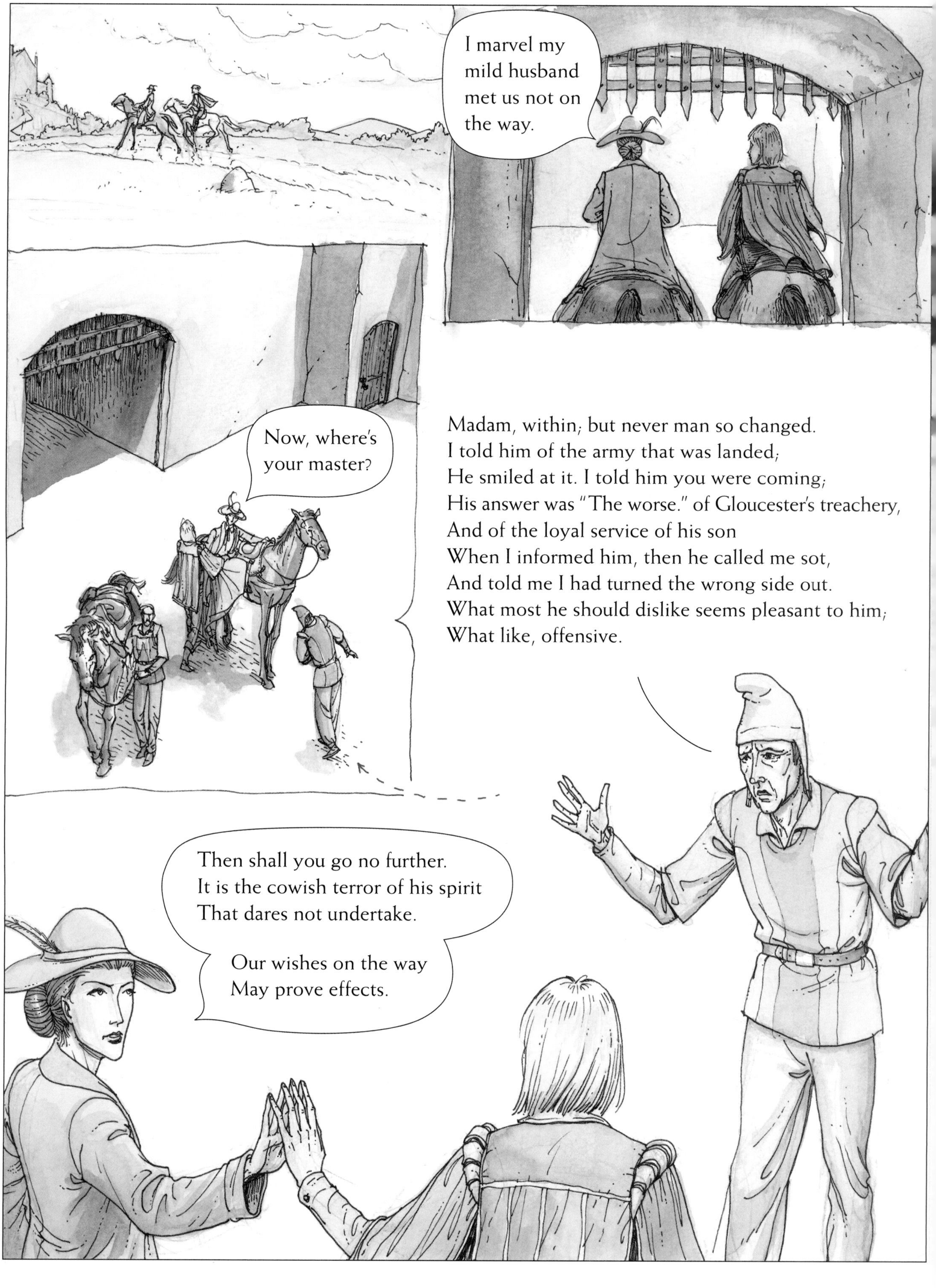
I marvel my mild husband met us not on the way.
Now, where's your master?
Madam, within; but never man so changed.
I told him of the army that was landed;
He smiled at it. I told him you were coming;
His answer was "The worse." of Gloucester's treachery,
And of the loyal service of his son
When I informed him, then he called me sot,
And told me I had turned the wrong side out.
What most he should dislike seems pleasant to him;
What like, offensive.
Then shall you go no further.
It is the cowish terror of his spirit
That dares not undertake.
Our wishes on the way
May prove effects.

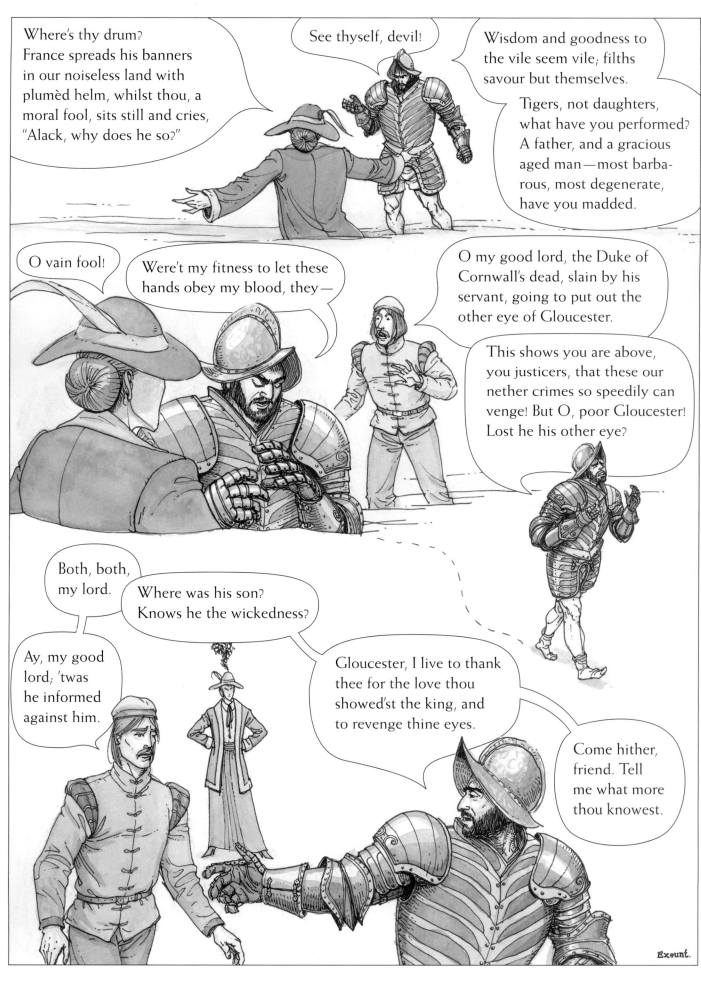

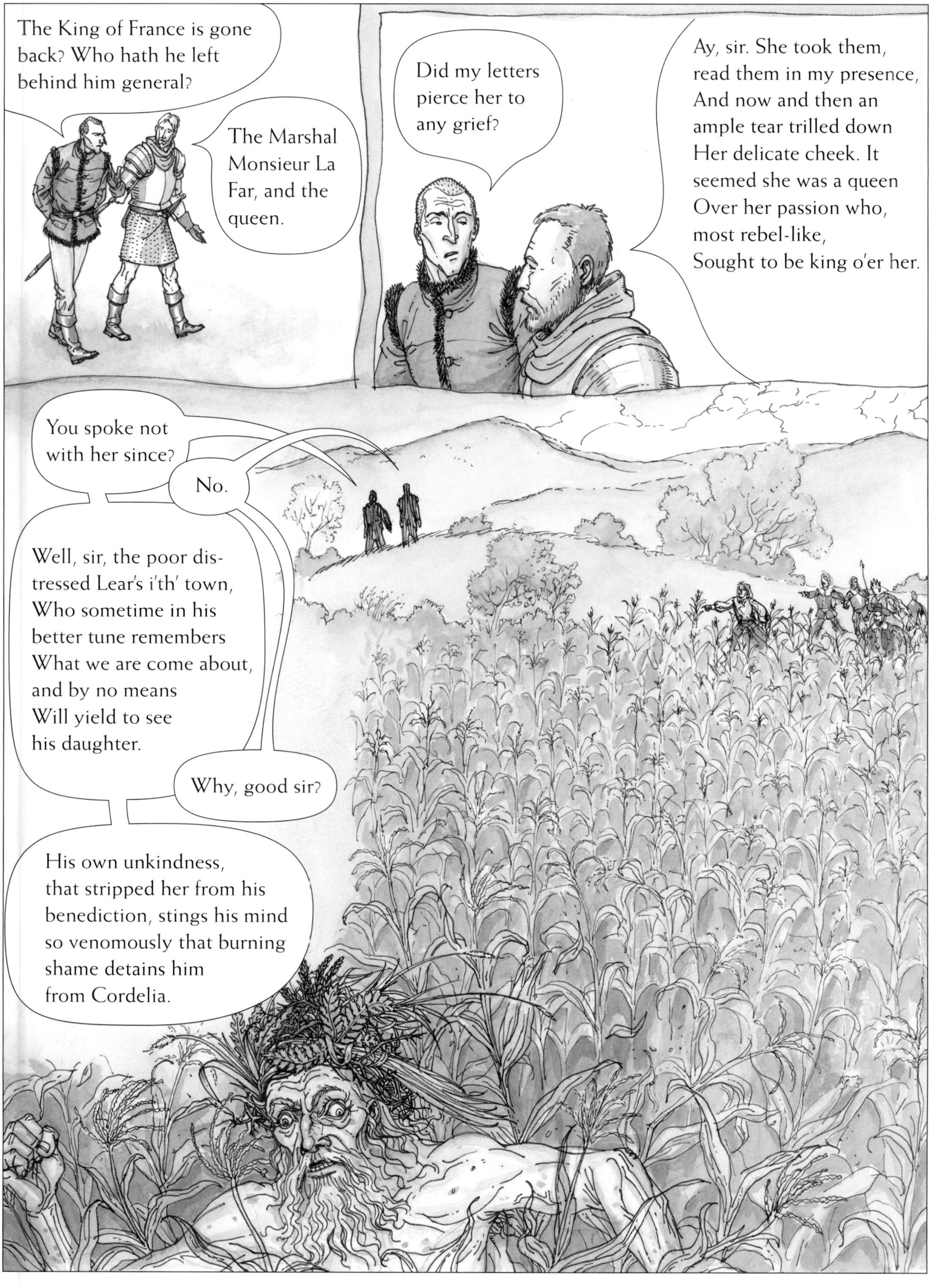

The King of France is gone back? Who hath he left behind him general?
The Marshal Monsieur La Far, and the queen.
Did my letters pierce her to any grief?
Ay, sir. She took them, read them in my presence, And now and then an ample tear trilled down Her delicate cheek. It seemed she was a queen Over her passion who, most rebel-like, Sought to be king o'er her.
You spoke not with her since?
No.
Well, sir, the poor distressed Lear's i'th' town, Who sometime in his better tune remembers What we are come about, and by no means Will yield to see his daughter.
Why, good sir?
His own unkindness, that stripped her from his benediction, stings his mind so venomously that burning shame detains him from Cordelia.

Search every acre in the high-grown field.
What can man's wisdom in restoring his bereavèd sense? He that helps him, take all my outward worth.
There is means, madam.
News, madam! The British powers are marching hitherward.
'Tis known; we stand in expectation of them.
O dear father, it is thy business that I go about. No blown ambition doth our arms incite, but love, dear love, and our aged father's right.
Soon may I hear and see him!
Are my brother's powers set forth?
Ay, madam.
Lord Edmund spake not with your lady at home?
No, madam.
What might import my sister's letter to him?
I know not, lady.

I know your lady does not love her husband, and at her late being here she gave most speaking looks to noble Edmund. I know you are of her bosom . . .

I, madam?

Therefore I do advise you, take note: my lord is dead. Edmund and I have talked, and more convenient is he for my hand than for your lady's.

If you do find him, pray you, give him this . . .

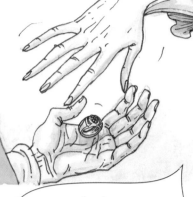

. . . and when your mistress hears thus much from you, I pray desire her call her wisdom to her.

So, fare you well. If you do chance to hear of that blind traitor, preferment falls on him that cuts him off.

When shall we come to the top of that hill?

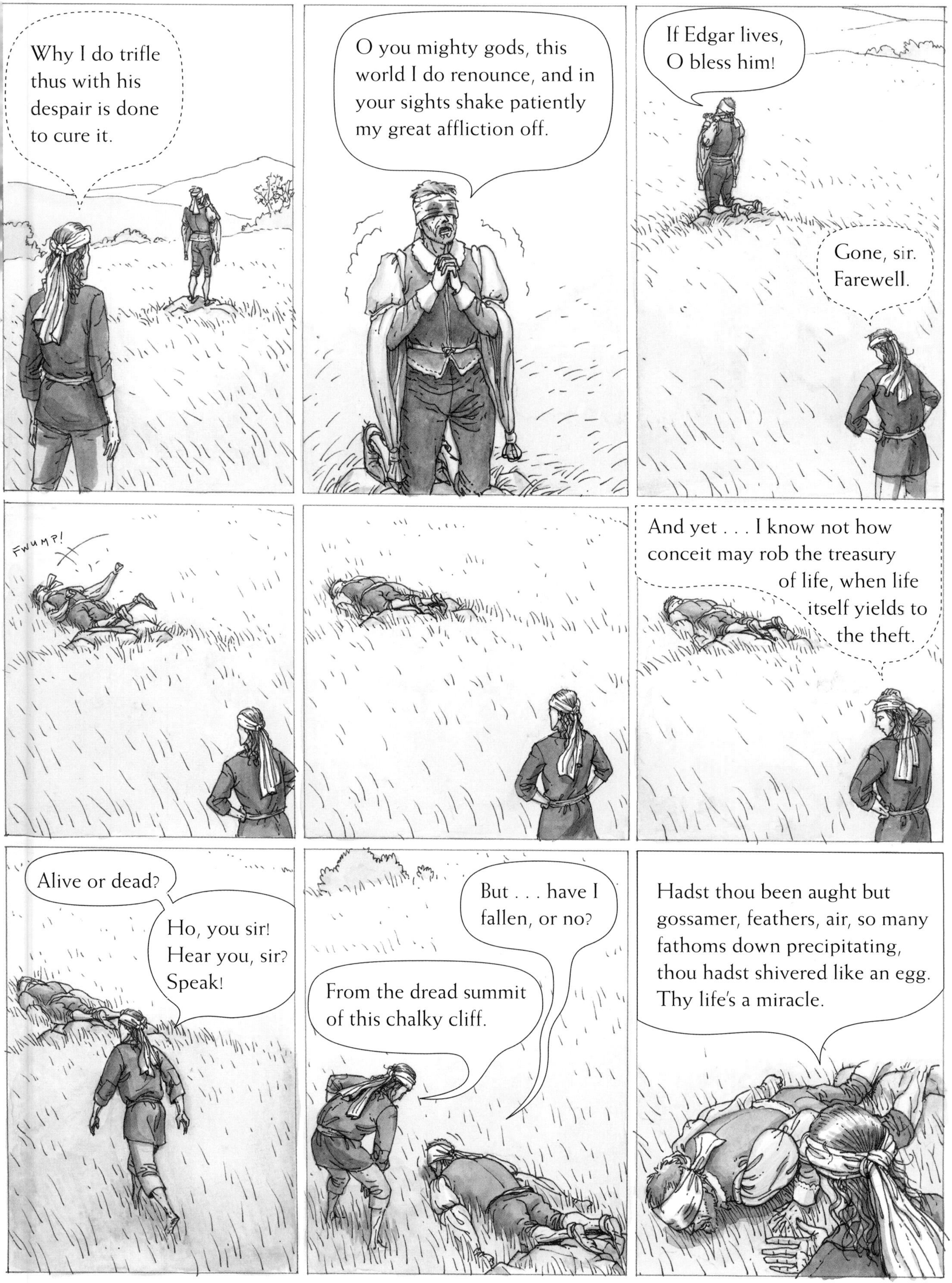
Why I do trifle thus with his despair is done to cure it.
O you mighty gods, this world I do renounce, and in your sights shake patiently my great affliction off.
If Edgar lives, O bless him!
Gone, sir. Farewell.
FWUMP!
And yet . . . I know not how conceit may rob the treasury of life, when life itself yields to the theft.
Alive or dead?
Ho, you sir! Hear you, sir? Speak!
But . . . have I fallen, or no?
From the dread summit of this chalky cliff.
Hadst thou been aught but gossamer, feathers, air, so many fathoms down precipitating, thou hadst shivered like an egg. Thy life's a miracle.

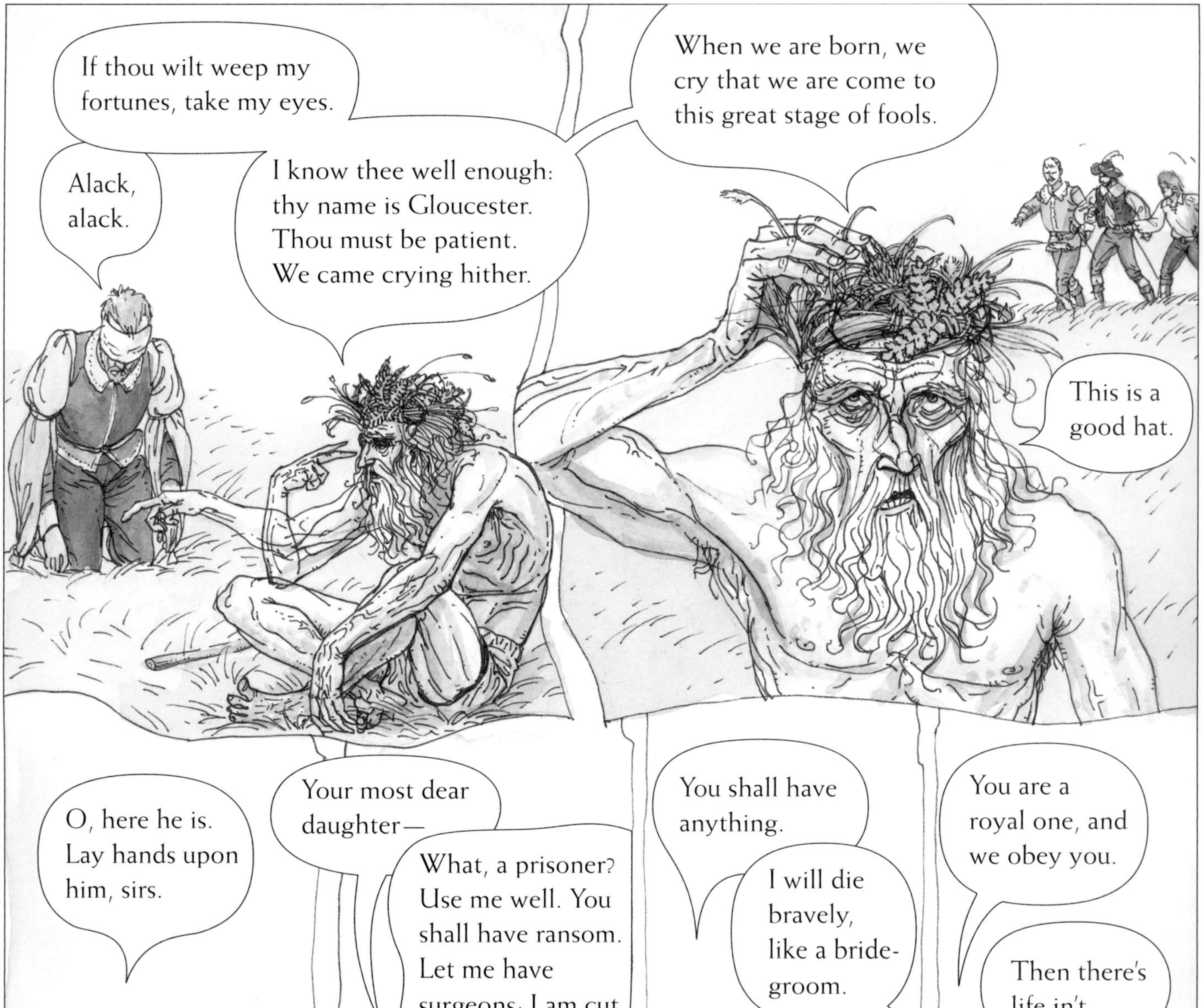

If thou wilt weep my fortunes, take my eyes.
Alack, alack.
I know thee well enough: thy name is Gloucester. Thou must be patient. We came crying hither.
When we are born, we cry that we are come to this great stage of fools.
This is a good hat.
O, here he is. Lay hands upon him, sirs.
Your most dear daughter—
What, a prisoner? Use me well. You shall have ransom. Let me have surgeons; I am cut to the brains.
You shall have anything.
I will die bravely, like a bride-groom.
You are a royal one, and we obey you.
Then there's life in't.
Come, an you get it, you shall get it with running.

84

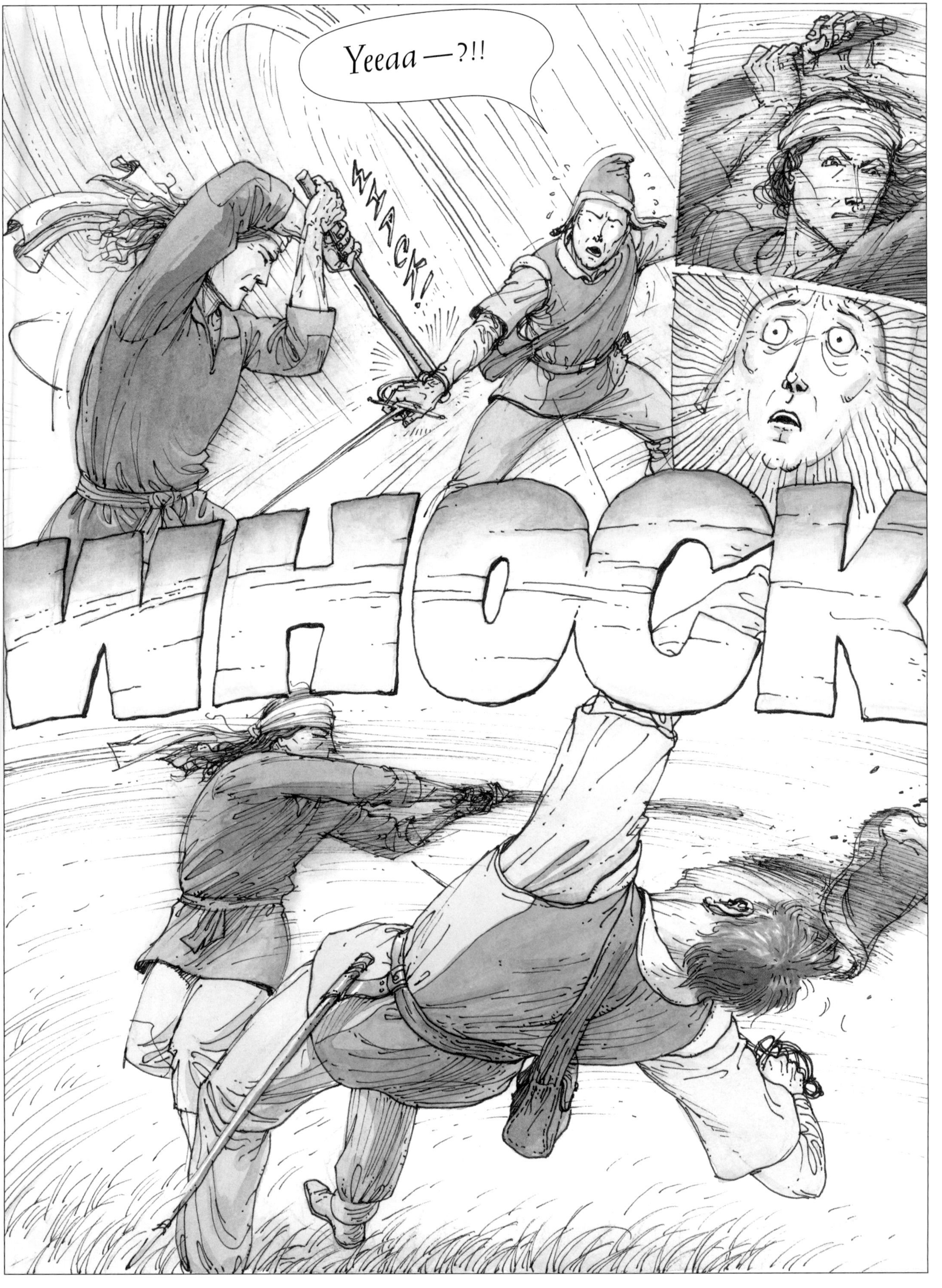
Yeeaa—?!!
WHACK!
WHOCK

Unh . . . Ngg—

Slave, thou hast slain me.

Villain, take my purse. If ever thou wilt thrive, bury my body, and give the letters which thou find'st about me to Edmund, Earl of Gloucester.

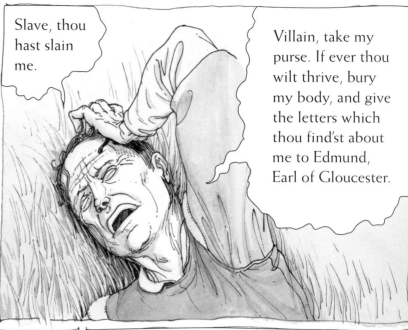

Seek him out among the British army.

O untimely death!

. . . ☀

I know thee well—a serviceable villain, as duteous to the vices of thy mistress as badness would desire.

What, is he dead?

Sit you down, father, rest you. Let's see his pockets. These letters that he speaks of may be my friends.

Leave, gentle wax; and manners blame us not. To know our enemies' minds, we'd rip their hearts; their papers is more lawful.

Let our reciprocal vows be rememb—
You have many opportunities to cut him off. If your will want not, time and place will be fruitfully offered. There is nothing done, if he return the conqueror; then am I the prisoner, and his bed my jail, from the loathed warmth whereof deliver me, and supply the place for your labour.

Your wife (so I would say),
Goneril ♡

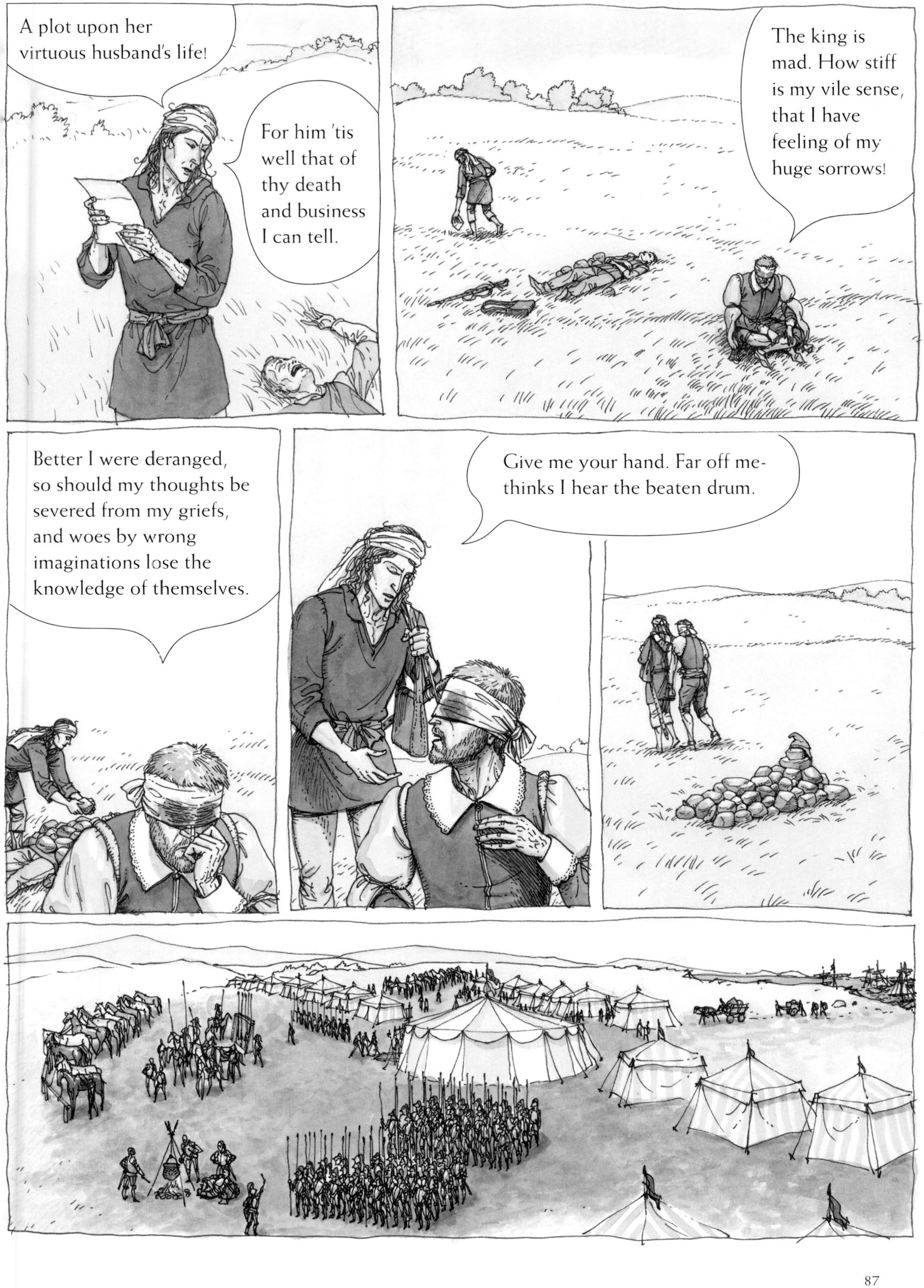
A plot upon her virtuous husband's life!
For him 'tis well that of thy death and business I can tell.
The king is mad. How stiff is my vile sense, that I have feeling of my huge sorrows!
Better I were deranged, so should my thoughts be severed from my griefs, and woes by wrong imaginations lose the knowledge of themselves.
Give me your hand. Far off me-thinks I hear the beaten drum.

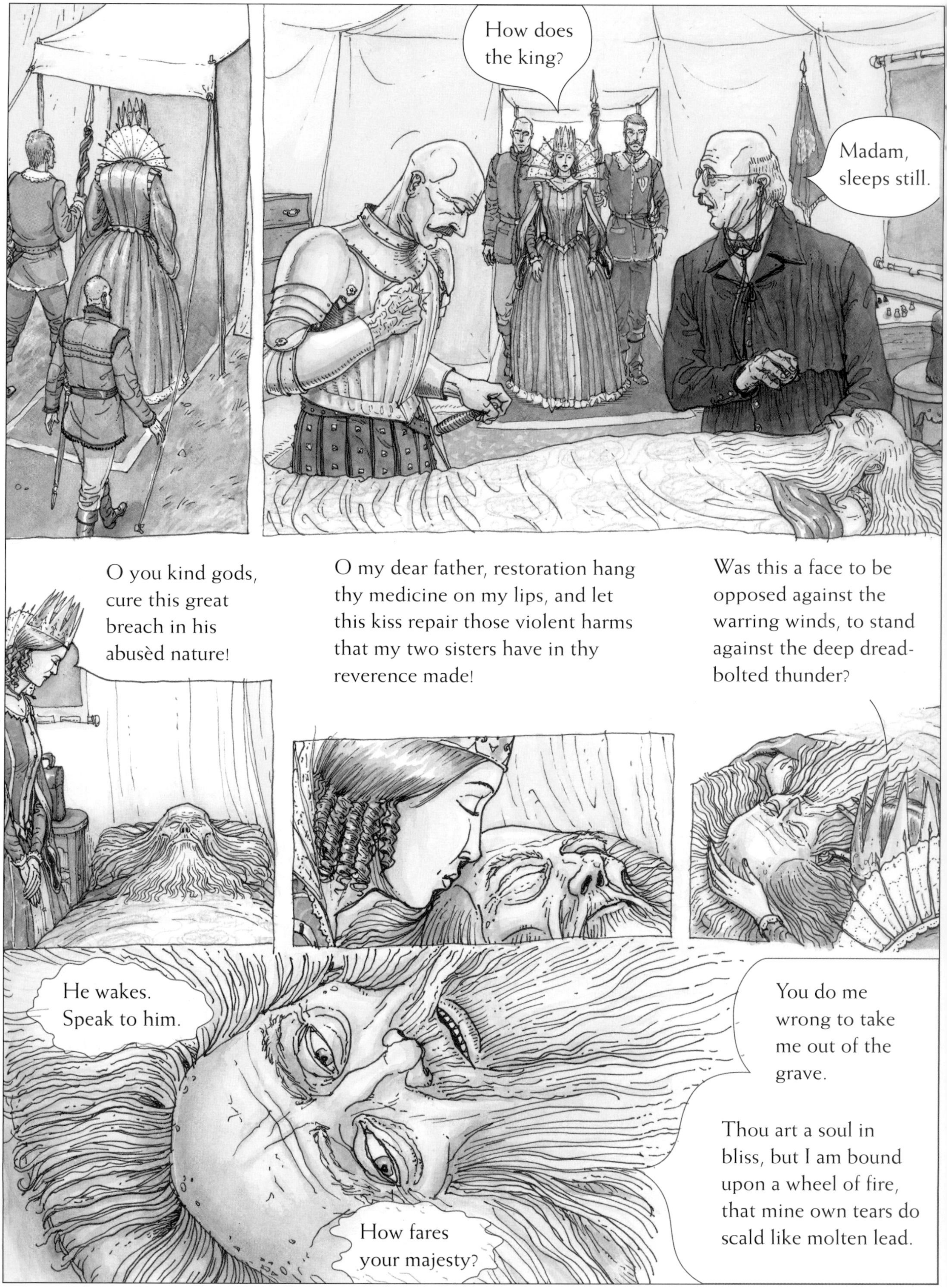
How does the king?
Madam, sleeps still.
O you kind gods, cure this great breach in his abusèd nature!
O my dear father, restoration hang thy medicine on my lips, and let this kiss repair those violent harms that my two sisters have in thy reverence made!
Was this a face to be opposed against the warring winds, to stand against the deep dread-bolted thunder?
He wakes. Speak to him.
How fares your majesty?
You do me wrong to take me out of the grave.
Thou art a soul in bliss, but I am bound upon a wheel of fire, that mine own tears do scald like molten lead.

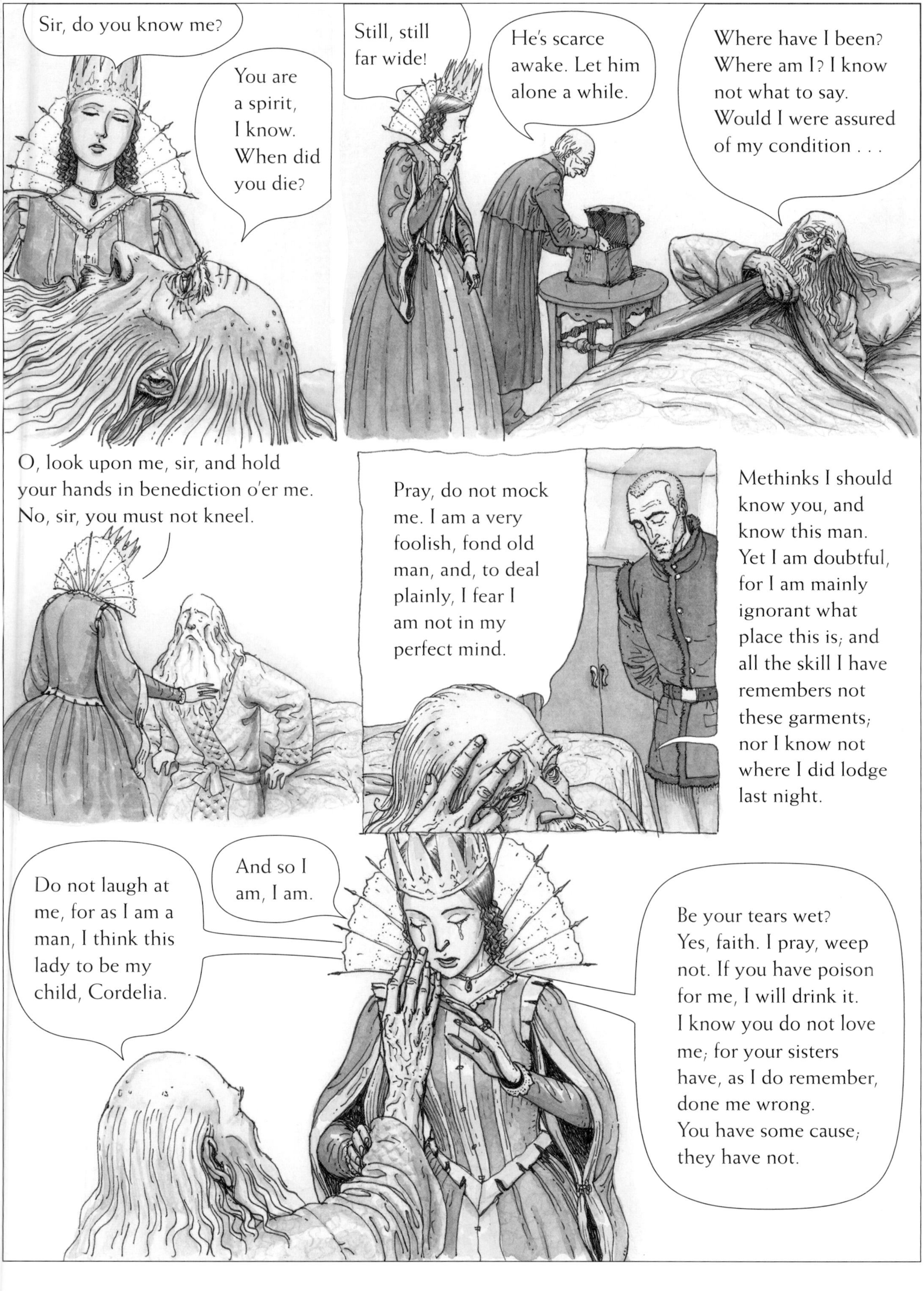
Sir, do you know me?
You are a spirit, I know. When did you die?
Still, still far wide!
He's scarce awake. Let him alone a while.
Where have I been? Where am I? I know not what to say. Would I were assured of my condition . . .
O, look upon me, sir, and hold your hands in benediction o'er me. No, sir, you must not kneel.
Pray, do not mock me. I am a very foolish, fond old man, and, to deal plainly, I fear I am not in my perfect mind.
Methinks I should know you, and know this man. Yet I am doubtful, for I am mainly ignorant what place this is; and all the skill I have remembers not these garments; nor I know not where I did lodge last night.
Do not laugh at me, for as I am a man, I think this lady to be my child, Cordelia.
And so I am, I am.
Be your tears wet? Yes, faith. I pray, weep not. If you have poison for me, I will drink it. I know you do not love me; for your sisters have, as I do remember, done me wrong. You have some cause; they have not.

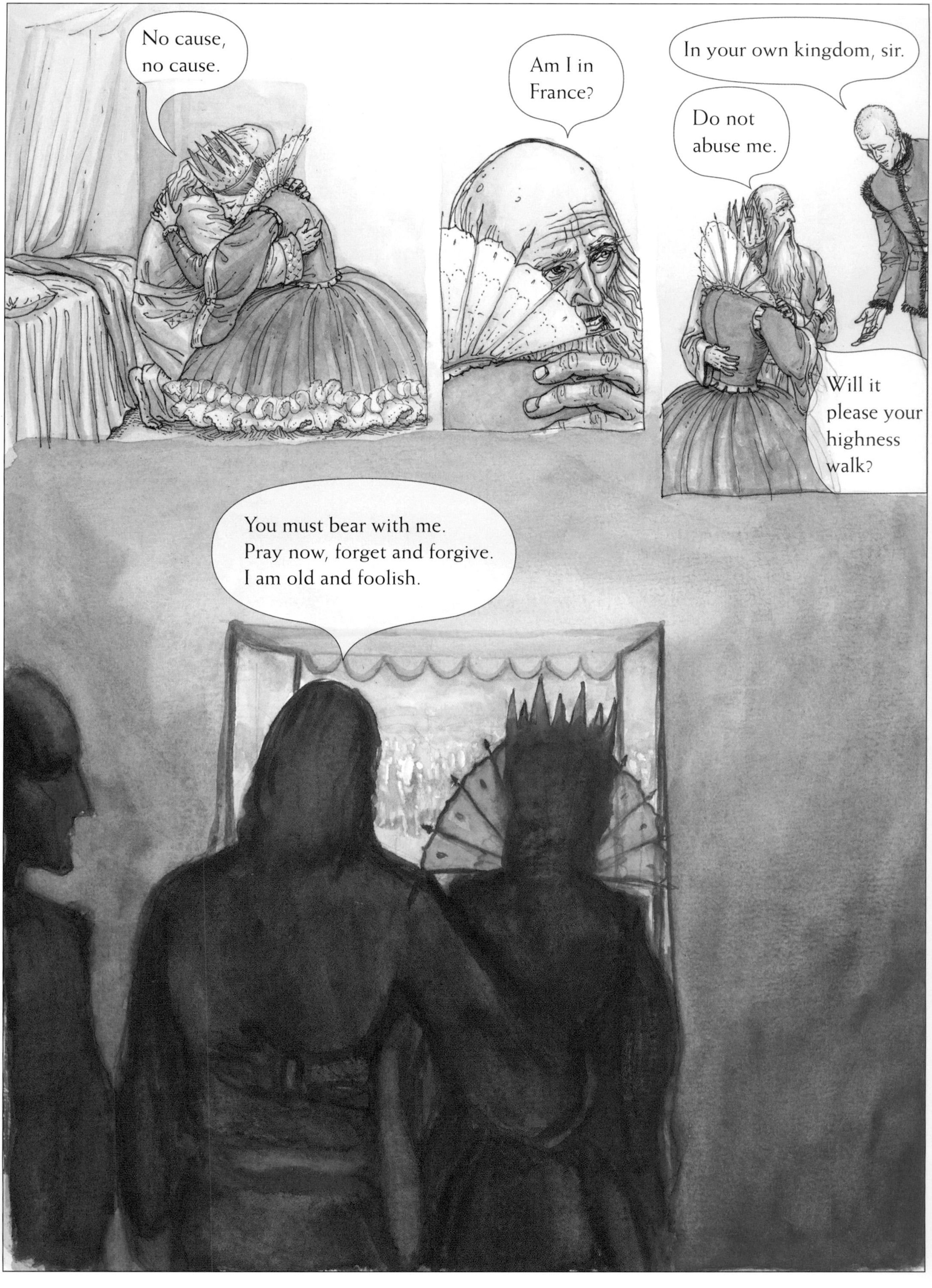
No cause,
no cause.
Am I in
France?
In your own kingdom, sir.
Do not
abuse me.
Will it
please your
highness
walk?
You must bear with me.
Pray now, forget and forgive.
I am old and foolish.

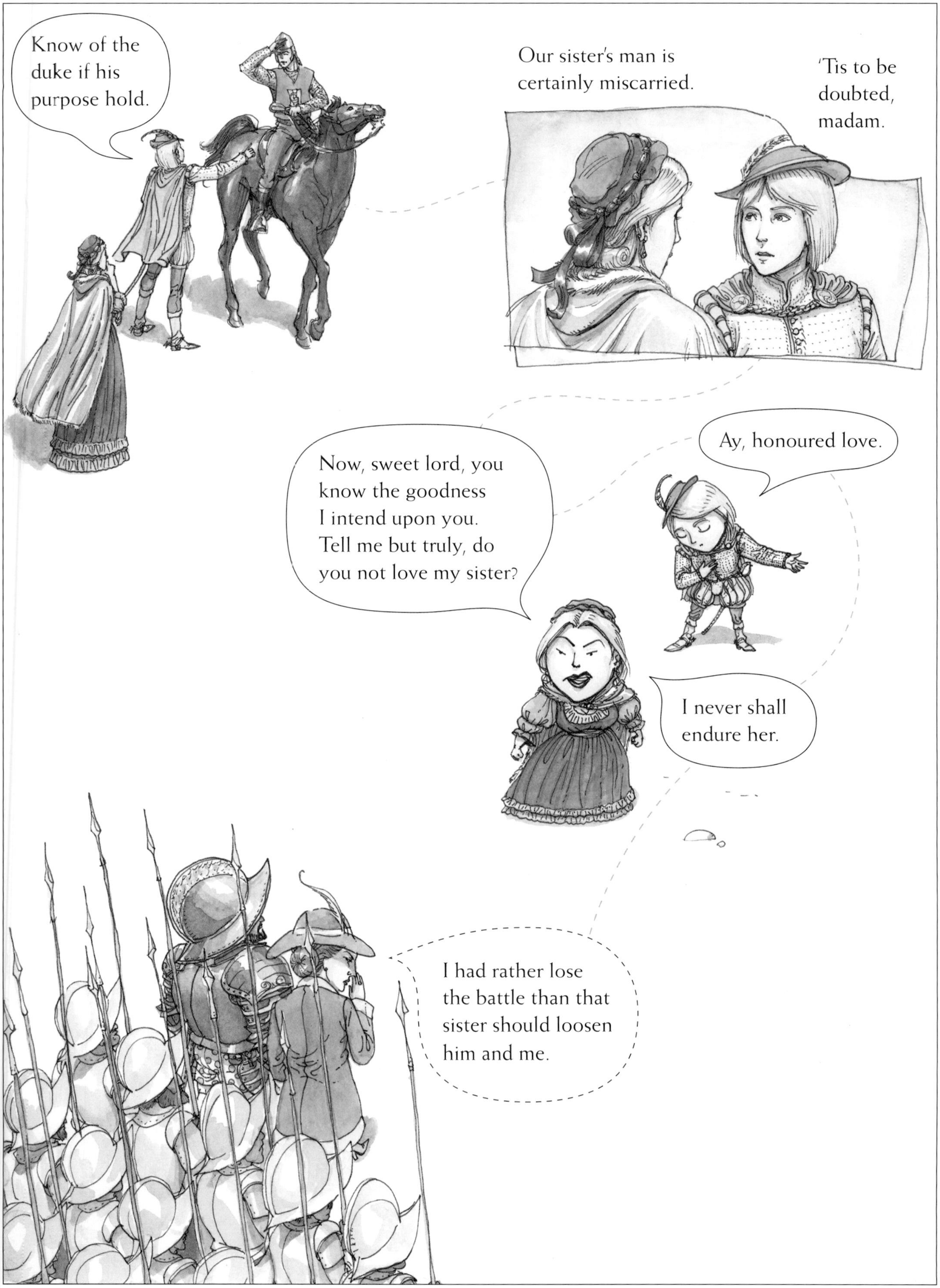
Know of the duke if his purpose hold.
Our sister's man is certainly miscarried.
'Tis to be doubted, madam.
Now, sweet lord, you know the goodness I intend upon you. Tell me but truly, do you not love my sister?
Ay, honoured love.
I never shall endure her.
I had rather lose the battle than that sister should loosen him and me.

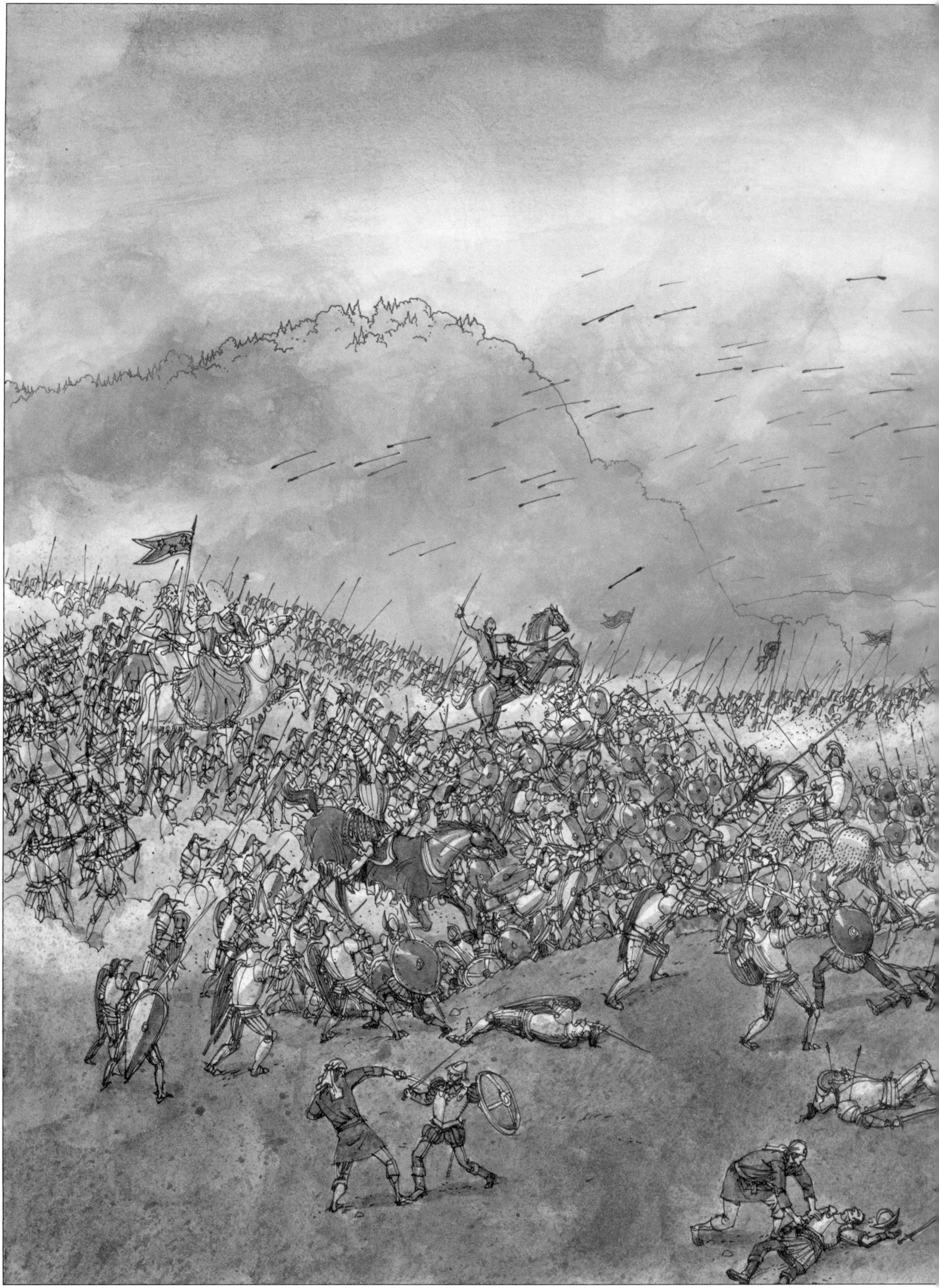

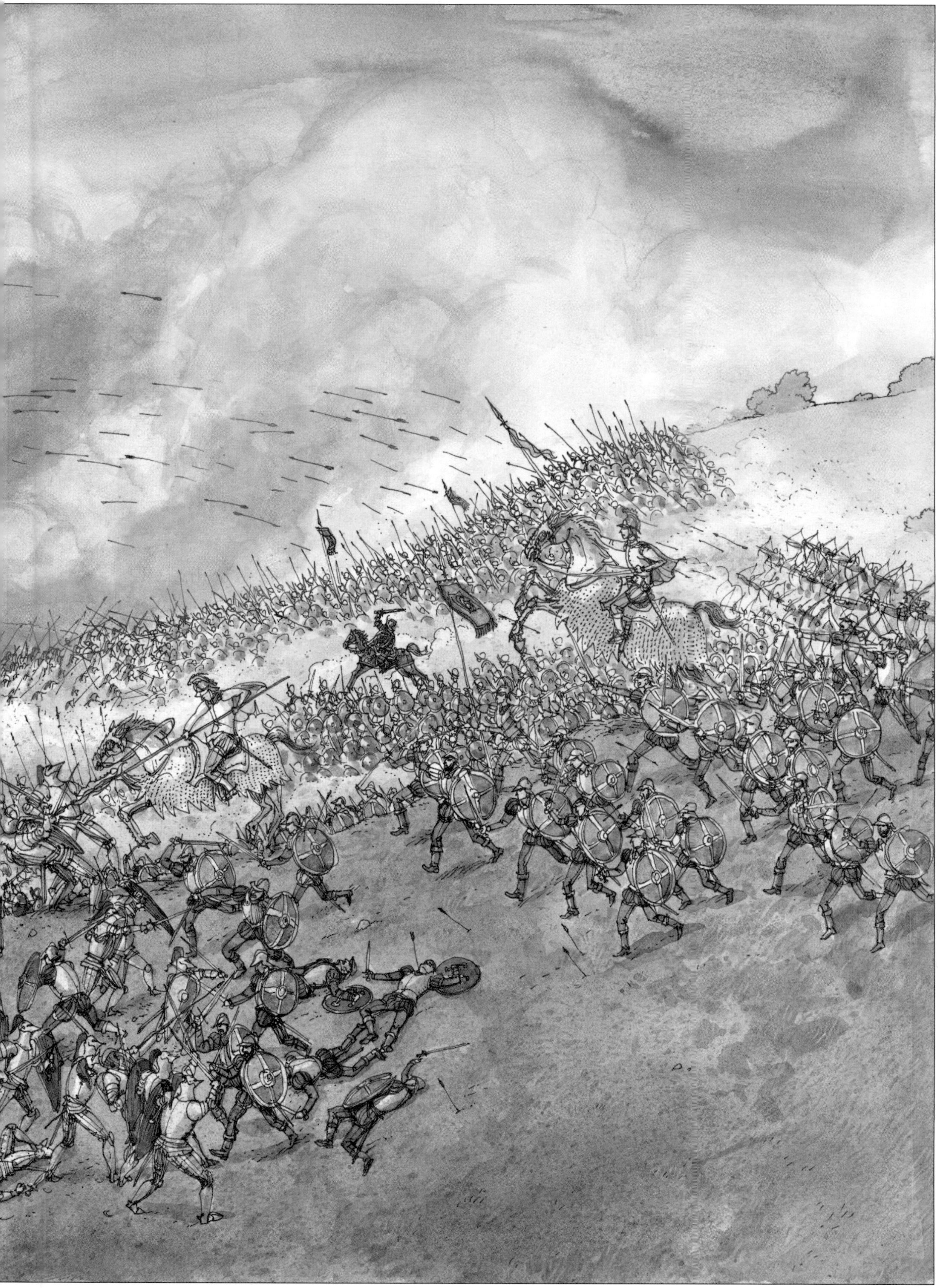

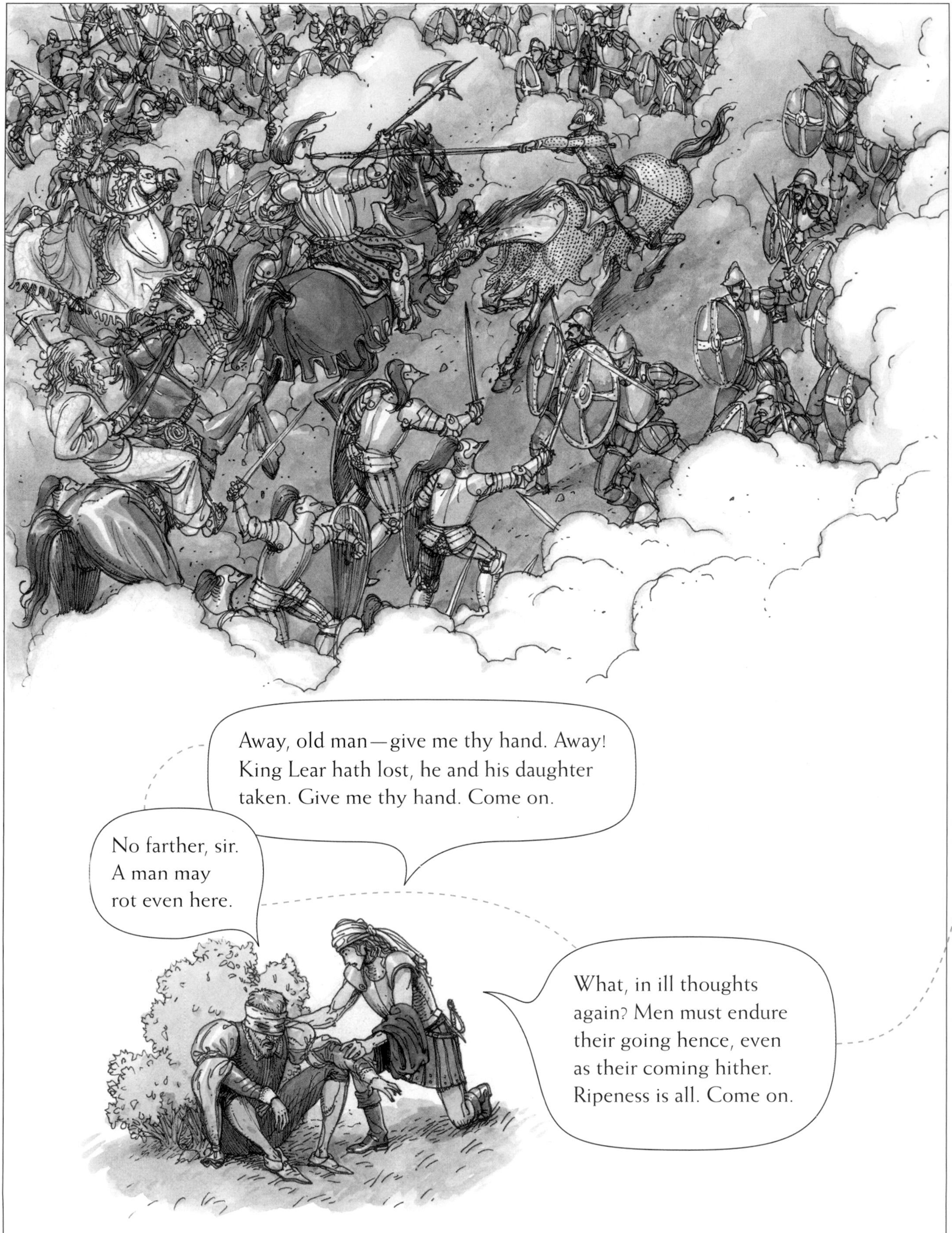
Away, old man—give me thy hand. Away! King Lear hath lost, he and his daughter taken. Give me thy hand. Come on.
No farther, sir. A man may rot even here.
What, in ill thoughts again? Men must endure their going hence, even as their coming hither. Ripeness is all. Come on.

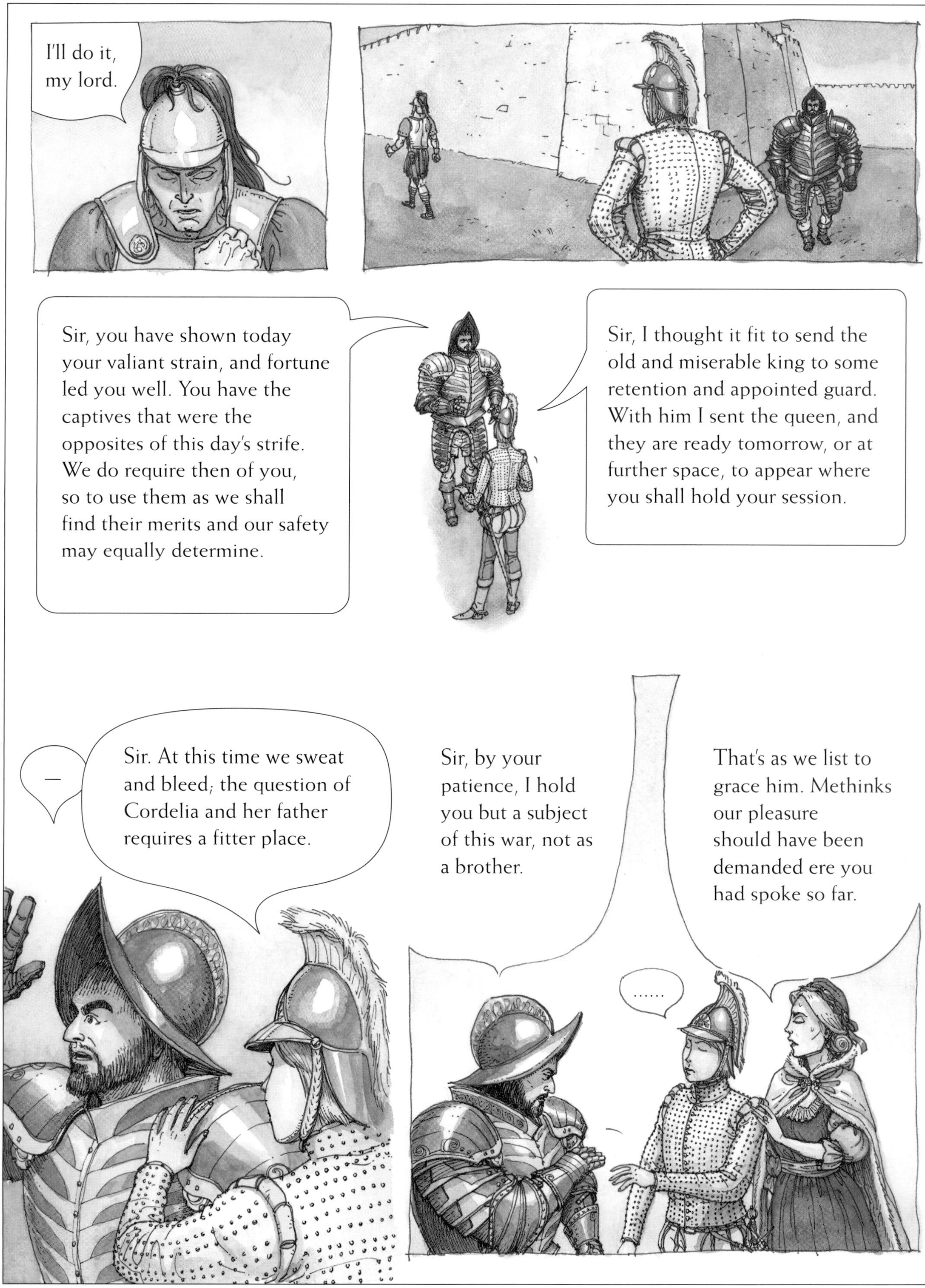
I'll do it, my lord.
Sir, you have shown today your valiant strain, and fortune led you well. You have the captives that were the opposites of this day's strife. We do require then of you, so to use them as we shall find their merits and our safety may equally determine.
Sir, I thought it fit to send the old and miserable king to some retention and appointed guard. With him I sent the queen, and they are ready tomorrow, or at further space, to appear where you shall hold your session.
—
Sir. At this time we sweat and bleed; the question of Cordelia and her father requires a fitter place.
Sir, by your patience, I hold you but a subject of this war, not as a brother.
That's as we list to grace him. Methinks our pleasure should have been demanded ere you had spoke so far.
......

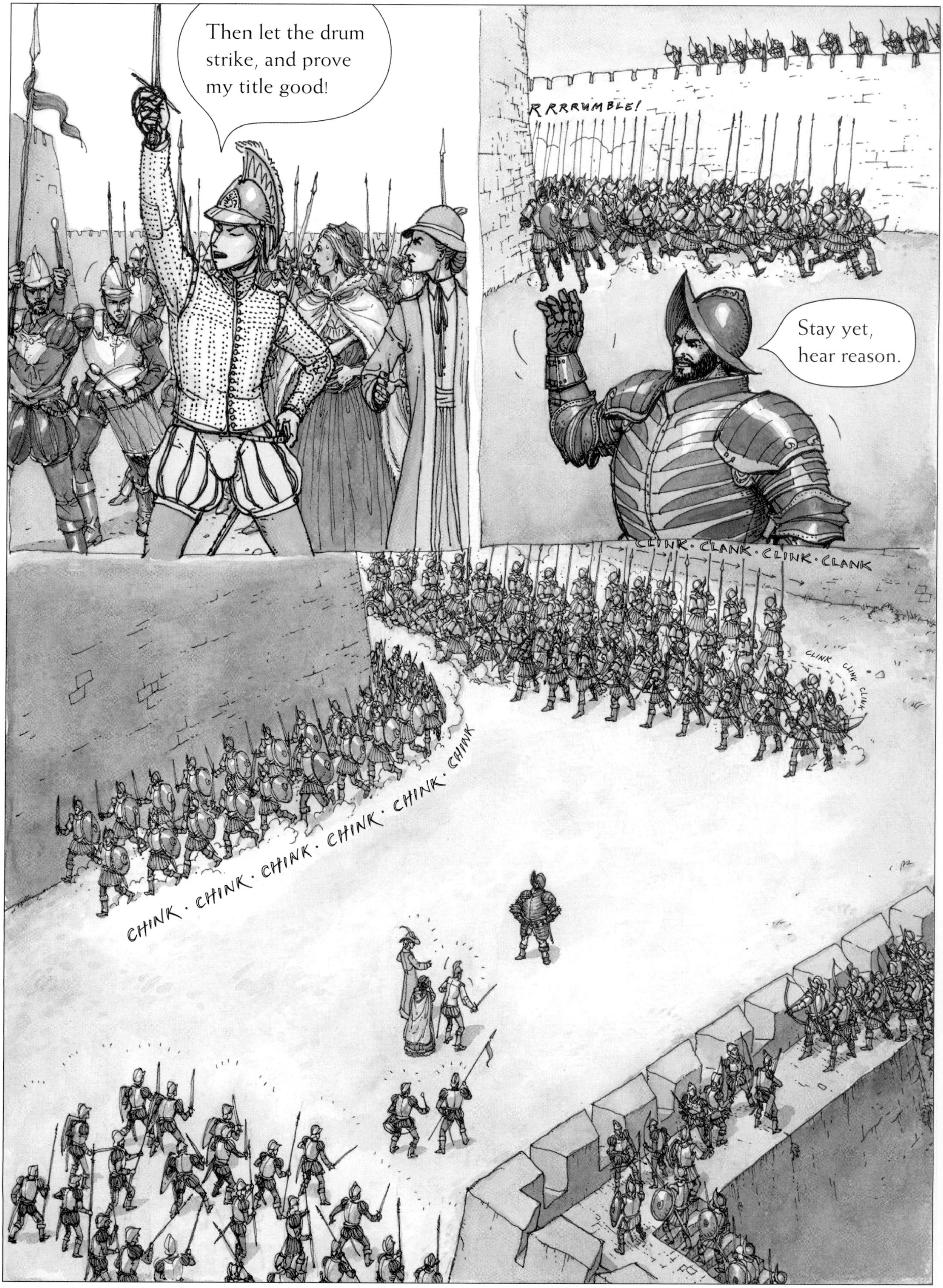
Then let the drum strike, and prove my title good!
RRRRUMBLE!
Stay yet, hear reason.
CLINK · CLANK · CLINK · CLANK
CLINK CLINK CLINK
CHINK · CHINK · CHINK · CHINK · CHINK · CHINK

Himself. What sayest thou to him?

Despite thy victor sword and fire-new fortune, thy valour and thy heart, thou art a traitor, false to thy gods, thy brother, and thy father, conspirant 'gainst this high illustrious prince, and from the extremest upward of thy head to the descent and dust beneath thy feet, a most toad-spotted traitor. Say thou no, this sword, this arm, and my best spirits are bent to prove upon thy heart, whereto I speak, thou liest.

In wisdom I should ask thy name; but since thy outside looks so fair and warlike, and that thy tongue some say of breeding breathes, what safe and nicely I might well demand by rule of knighthood, I disdain and spurn. Back do I toss these treasons to thy head, with the hell-hated lie o'erwhelm thy heart, which, for they yet glance by and scarcely bruise, this sword of mine shall give them instant way where they shall rest forever.

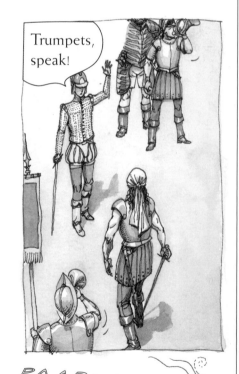

Trumpets, speak!

PARAAAAAAAAA

PAARUMPAAAAAAA

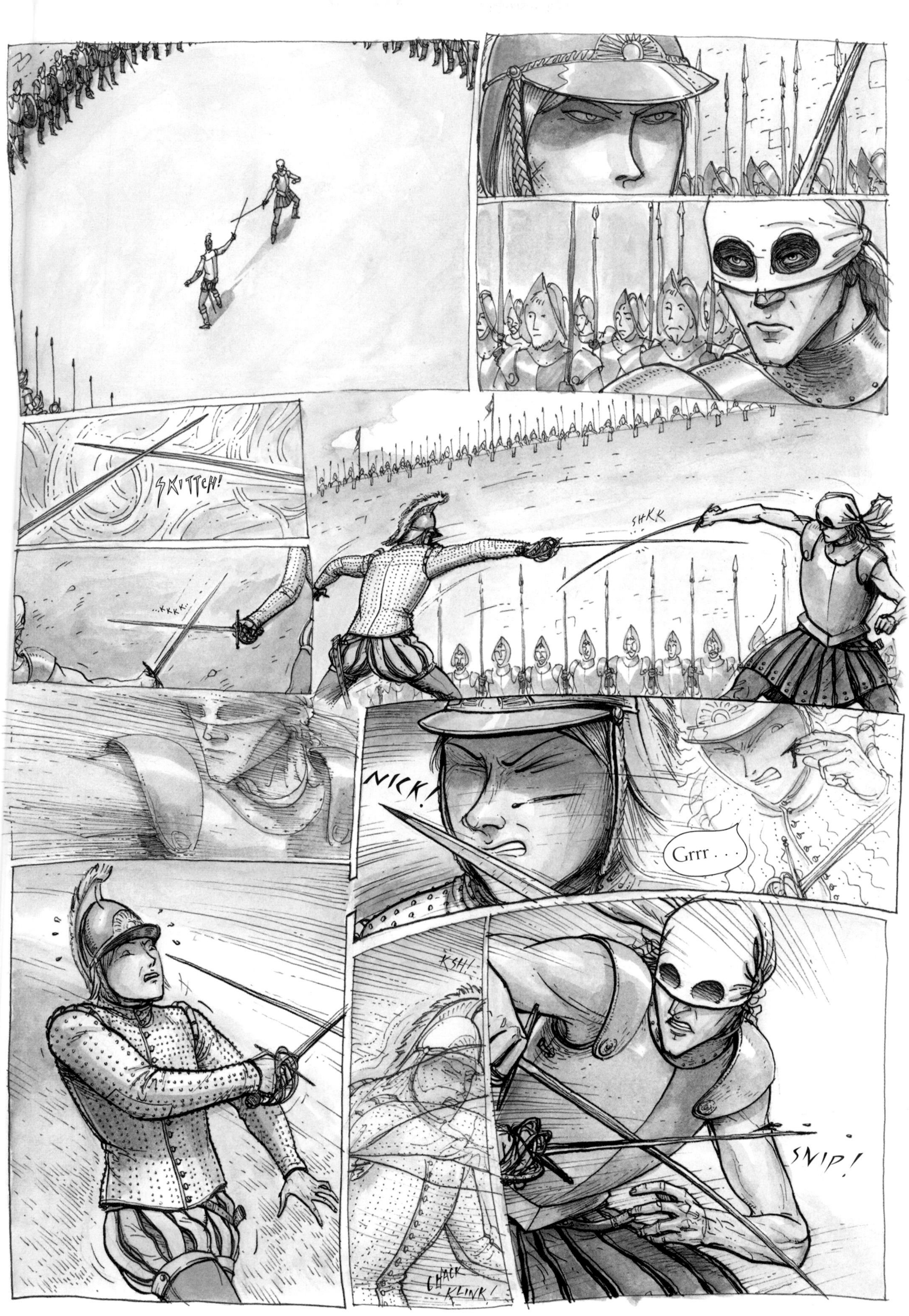
SKITTCH!
...KKKK.
SHKK
NICK!
Grrr . . .
KSH!
SNIP!
CHACK
KLINK!

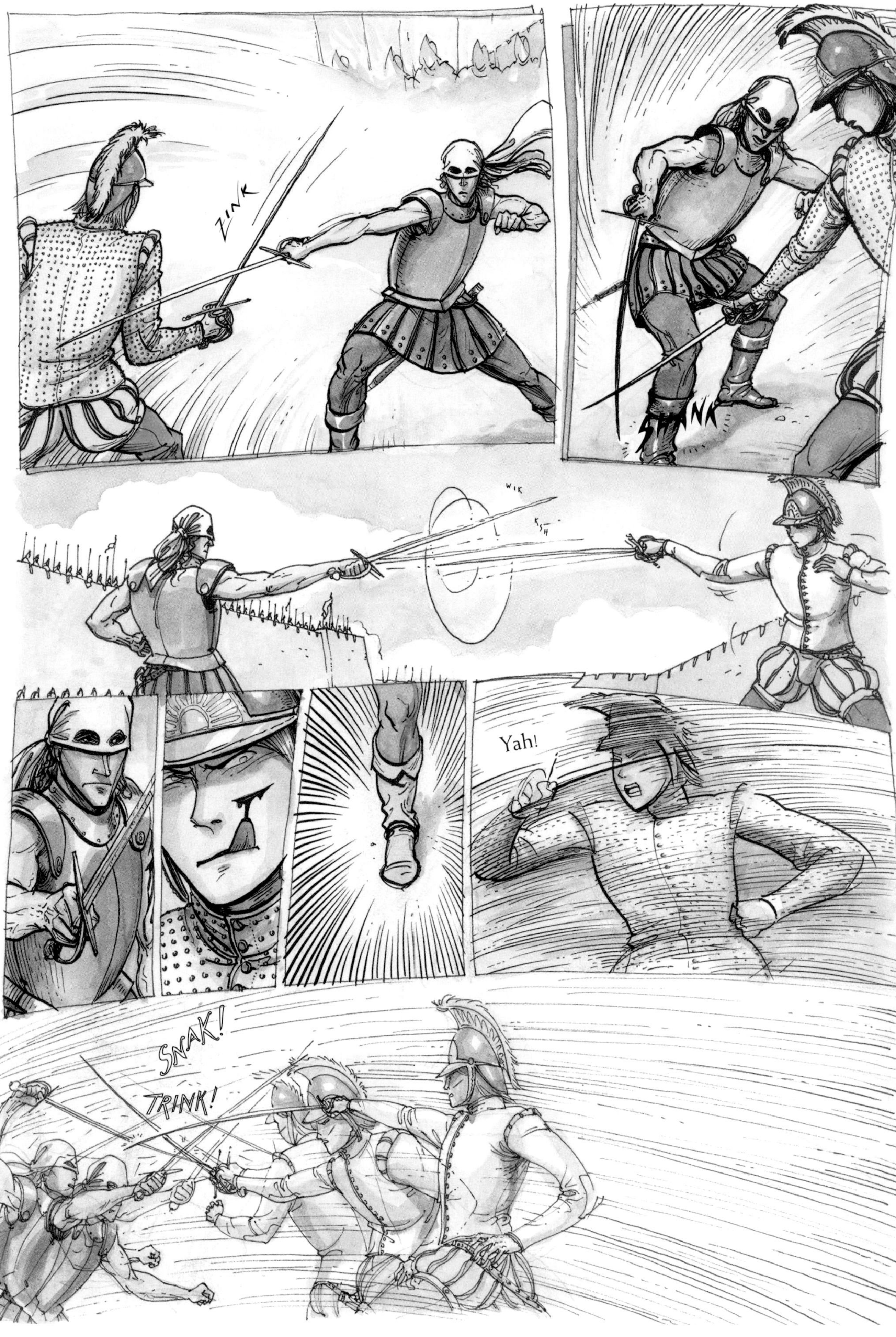
ZINK
SHANK
WIK
KSH
Yah!
SNAK!
TRINK!

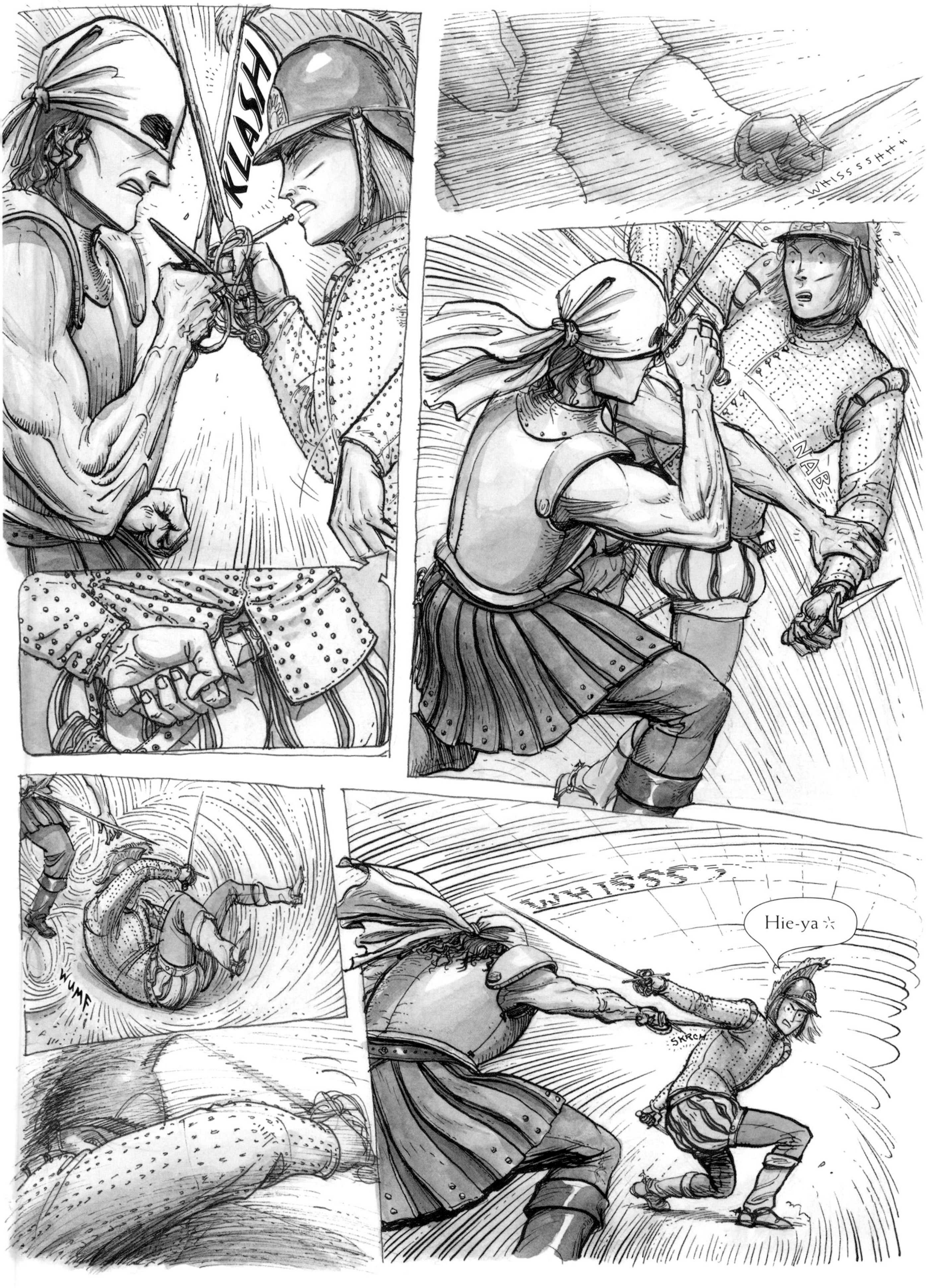
KLASH
WHISSSSSHHH
NAB
WUMF
Hie-ya ☆
SKRCH

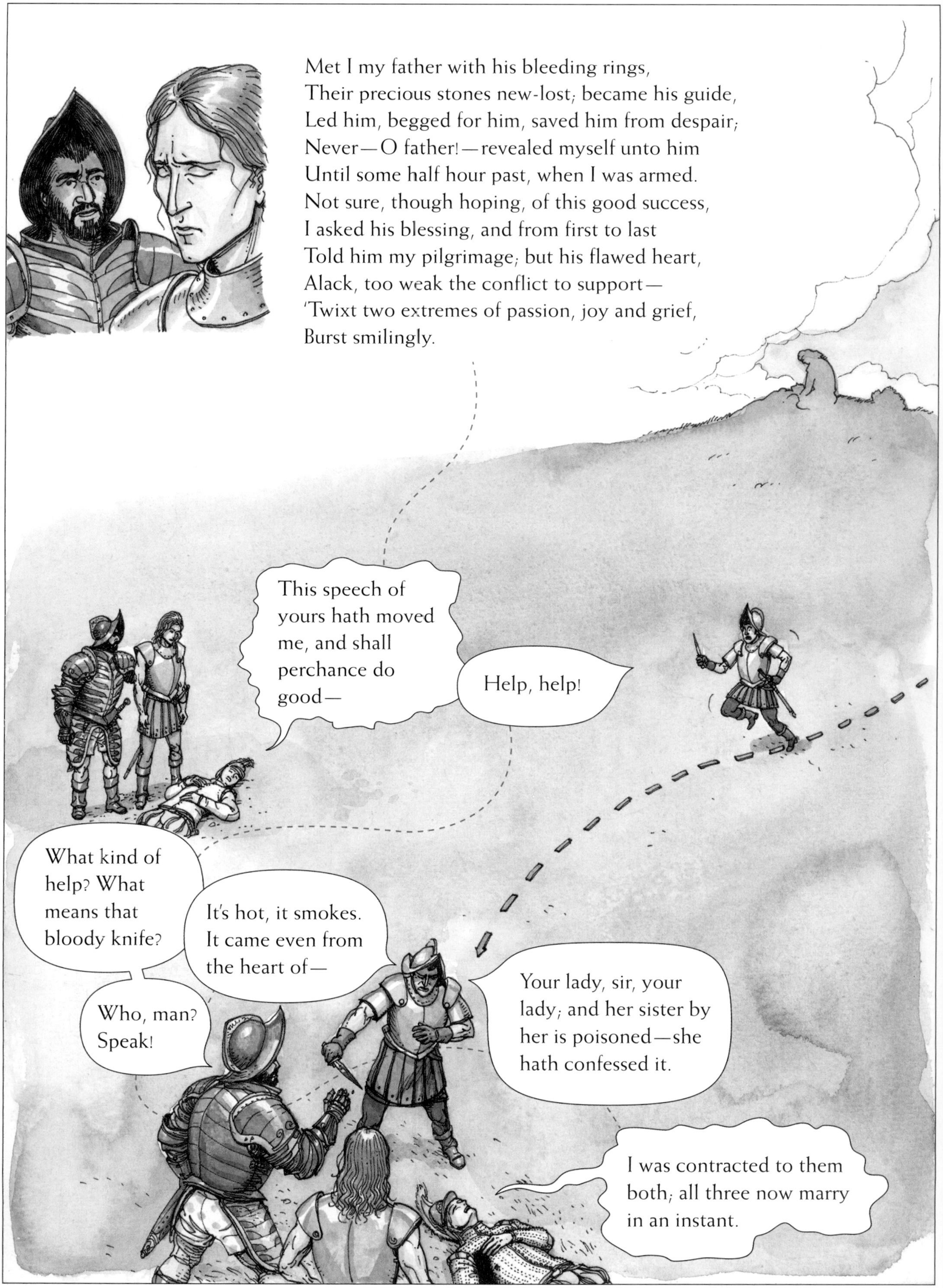

Met I my father with his bleeding rings,
Their precious stones new-lost; became his guide,
Led him, begged for him, saved him from despair;
Never—O father!—revealed myself unto him
Until some half hour past, when I was armed.
Not sure, though hoping, of this good success,
I asked his blessing, and from first to last
Told him my pilgrimage; but his flawed heart,
Alack, too weak the conflict to support—
'Twixt two extremes of passion, joy and grief,
Burst smilingly.
This speech of yours hath moved me, and shall perchance do good—
Help, help!
What kind of help? What means that bloody knife?
It's hot, it smokes. It came even from the heart of—
Who, man? Speak!
Your lady, sir, your lady; and her sister by her is poisoned—she hath confessed it.
I was contracted to them both; all three now marry in an instant.

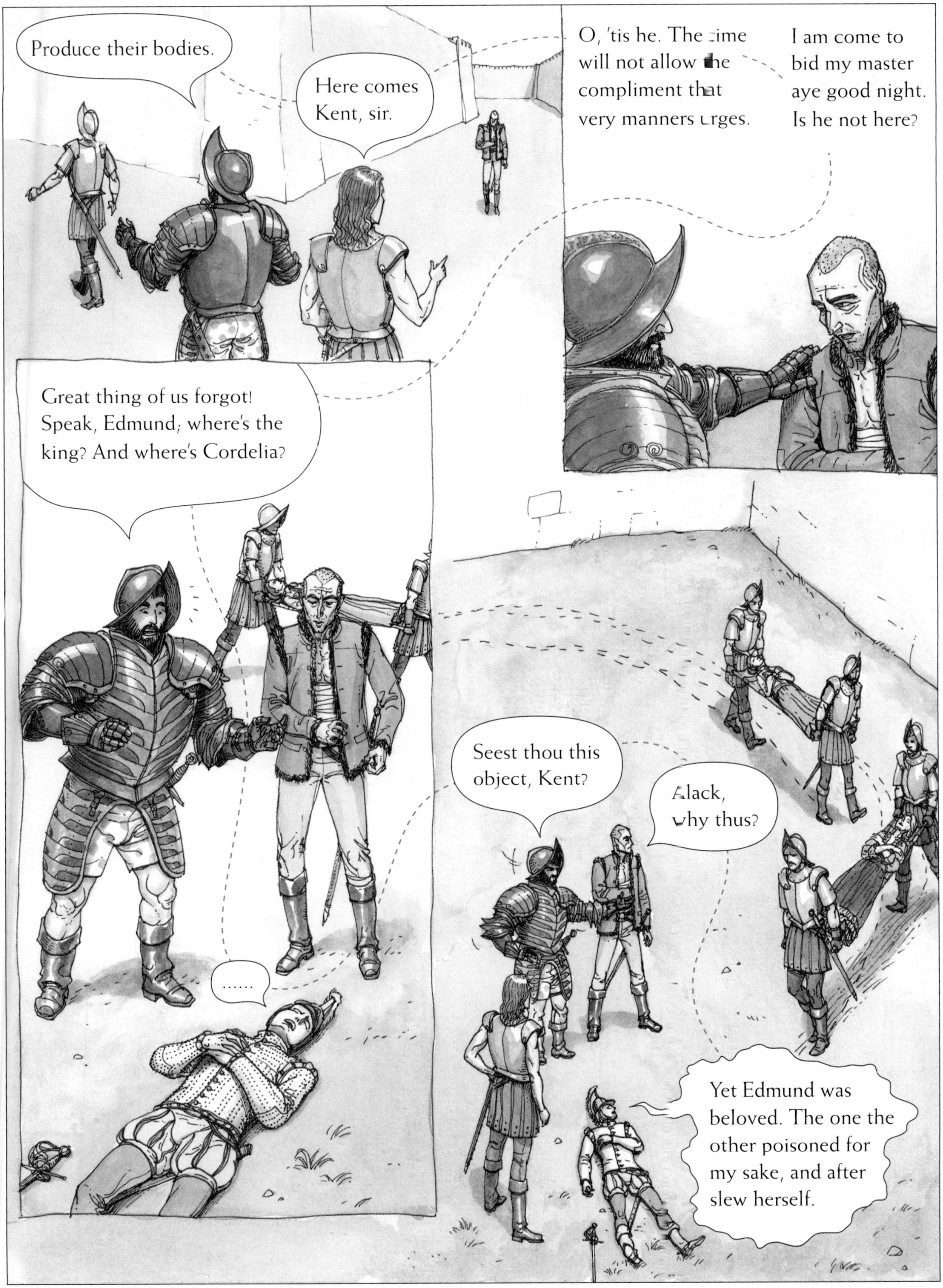

Produce their bodies.
Here comes Kent, sir.
O, 'tis he. The time will not allow the compliment that very manners urges.
I am come to bid my master aye good night. Is he not here?
Great thing of us forgot! Speak, Edmund; where's the king? And where's Cordelia?
......
Seest thou this object, Kent?
Alack, why thus?
Yet Edmund was beloved. The one the other poisoned for my sake, and after slew herself.

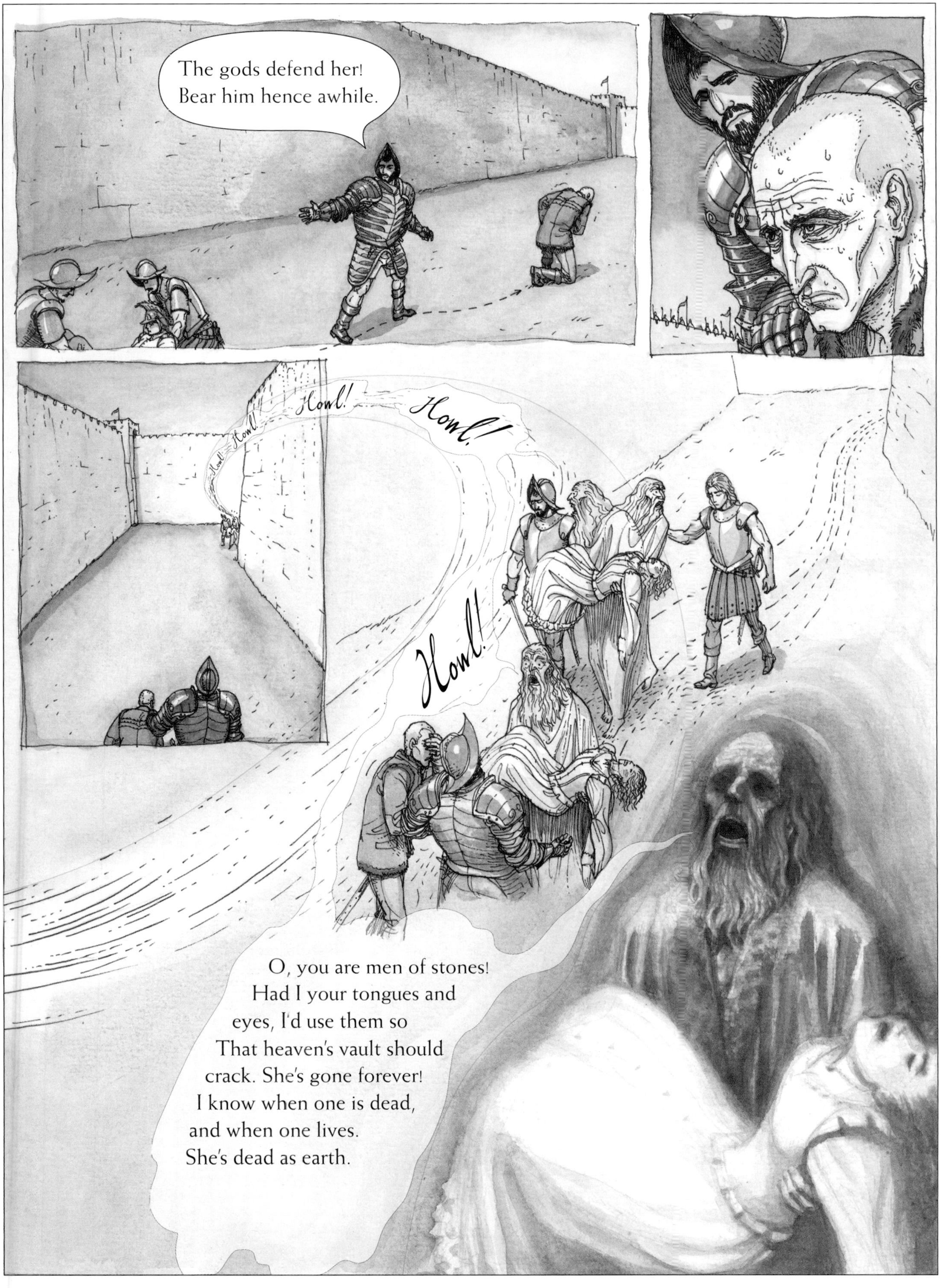
The gods defend her! Bear him hence awhile.
Howl! Howl! Howl! Howl!
Howl!
O, you are men of stones! Had I your tongues and eyes, I'd use them so That heaven's vault should crack. She's gone forever! I know when one is dead, and when one lives. She's dead as earth.

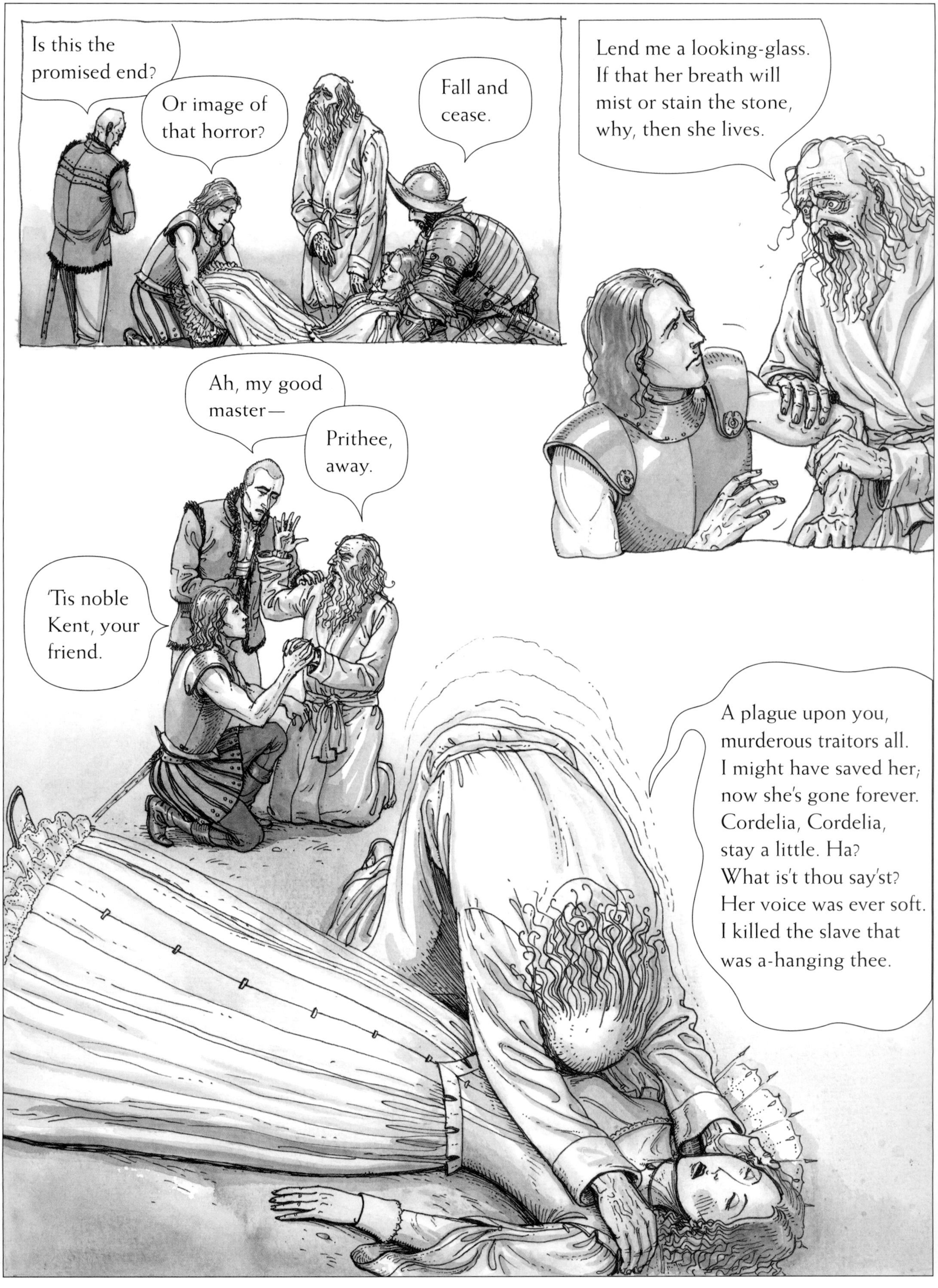
Is this the promised end?
Or image of that horror?
Fall and cease.
Lend me a looking-glass. If that her breath will mist or stain the stone, why, then she lives.
Ah, my good master—
Prithee, away.
'Tis noble Kent, your friend.
A plague upon you, murderous traitors all. I might have saved her; now she's gone forever. Cordelia, Cordelia, stay a little. Ha? What is't thou say'st? Her voice was ever soft. I killed the slave that was a-hanging thee.

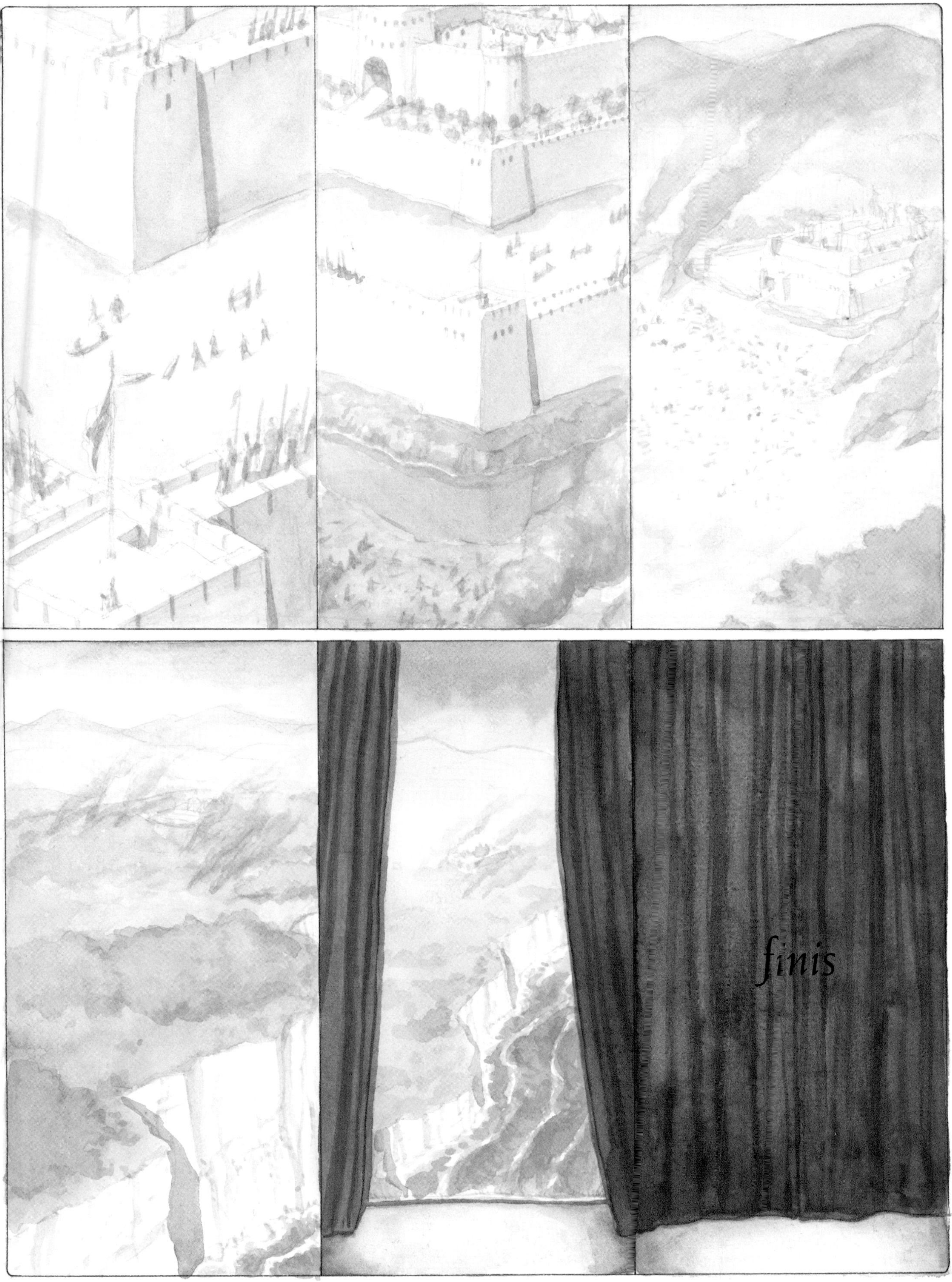
finis

*In memory of my teacher
David Passalacqua and of my grandfather, Mel*

I would like to thank all of my friends who proofread various drafts or gave me feedback during the epic course of this project: Paul, Lydia, Sean, Lynda, Dan and Laurie, Cat and Josh, Wes, Gretchen, Bill, Mat and Dianne, my wonderful and supportive parents, and my Shakespeare expert, Sarah. I'd also like to thank my "team" at Candlewick Press: Deb, Heather, and Sherry, plus Gregg, Jen, Laura, Anne, Sharon, and all the other lovely folks there who help to produce and market my books. But most of all, I'd like to thank my tireless and loving co-conspirator, Alison.

NOTES

Shakespeare's plays were first published as a series of Quartos (small paperbacks) and then collected into a larger, more prestigious Folio volume. As a rule, the Quarto and Folio editions vary little, but in the case of *King Lear,* there are numerous differences, including whole scenes that appear in only one or the other. Most modern editions of *Lear* are conflated texts, based primarily on the Folio but with scenes from the Quarto added. I found that I preferred the Quarto, so I began there, adding selections from the Folio as appropriate.

Much of the play is written in iambic pentameter. Although in some of the important speeches I was able to preserve the original verse line breaks, more often I had to remove them and set the text as prose to maintain the flow of the dialogue. Sometimes, too, I split lines or changed a particularly archaic word. In each of these cases I carefully considered the meter and broke it only if I felt the impact was minimal.

Shakespeare's writing is remarkably rich. Every word of the original play reveals something about its themes, symbols, or characters. But to adapt *King Lear* to the graphic novel format, I had to cut a lot of material inessential to the narrative. These notes explain alterations I made and offer insight into the themes or ideas explored in some of the absent passages. I hope that the notes will also help to illustrate the depth of this play, as well as the challenges and opportunities involved in retelling it.

PAGE 1: Note the eclipse, which Gloucester refers to on page 13. A recurring theme of the play is the question of whether astronomical phenomena affect human actions or destinies.

PAGE 2: I've shortened this exchange between Gloucester, Edmund, and Kent. In the original text, Gloucester makes another joke about Edmund's illegitimate parentage, and Edmund and Kent exchange courtesies. The most notable line is Edmund's "Sir, I shall study deserving." Deserving does not come naturally to Edmund, and he is only academically interested in it.

PAGES 2–4: Shakespeare's text gives no indication as to whether Lear's map is pre-divided or not. The play is often performed using a pre-divided map, which makes Lear's "test" for his daughters a sham (no matter how flattering their speeches, their shares are already determined, as Lear assumes that all of his daughters are suitably obedient). I chose to leave the illustrations ambiguous on this point. I also chose to have the map depict America, mainly to establish that I'm taking liberties with the play's historical grounding.

PAGE 5: "Nothing" is a central theme in the play and makes its first appearance here as the spark that ignites Lear's anger.

PAGE 12: Note the use of "nothing" again.

PAGE 15: In the last panel, I cut two lines: Lear says, "What's that?" and Kent replies, "Authority." The nature of authority is another big theme in this play.

PAGE 19: More references to "nothing."

In the original text, the fool has several more choice words for Lear, continuing to mock him for dividing his crown.

PAGE 22: I cut a nice section here in which Goneril chides Albany for his "milky gentleness."

PAGE 32: For the sake of a better visual transition to Edgar, I've cut a section in which Kent takes out a letter from Cordelia and peruses it, which establishes that they are in communication and may be plotting something.

PAGE 50: I cut "the younger rises when the old doth fall," which is a nice statement of another recurring theme.

PAGE 51: There were two pieces of Lear's dialogue I considered using on this page, but I couldn't fit them both. I chose the one that I think is more thematically important and sacrificed "Thou think'st 'tis much that this contentious storm / Invades us to the skin. So 'tis to thee. But where the greater malady is fixed, / The lesser is scarce felt."

PAGE 53: I cut Edgar's fictitious origin ("A serving-man, proud in heart and mind . . . that slept in the contriving of lust, and waked to do it"), which is entertaining in its own right and is possibly intended to ape Oswald.

PAGE 55: I cut a nice little speech by Gloucester about the betrayal by his son, which highlights the parallels between his story and Lear's. I think the parallels are clear enough without that passage.

PAGE 64: Another major theme is this play is (in)justice. It makes a direct appearance in this scene when Cornwall says,

"Pinion him like a thief; bring him before us. / Though we may not pass upon his life / Without the form of justice, yet our power / Shall do a curtsy to our wrath, which men / May blame but not control."

PAGE 65: *True* is used here to mean loyal, but elsewhere in the play it is used by other characters to show various meanings and perceptions of truth. For example, Cordelia's "so young, my lord, and true," Lear's "thy truth then be thy dower," and Cornwall's "True or false, it hath made thee Earl of Gloucester."

PAGE 71: In order to fit this scene on one page, I had to cut a lot of dialogue. Edgar begins the original scene with a rather long monologue, the gist of which is that things can't get any worse: "The lamentable change is from the best; / The worst returns to laughter." He repents voicing such a sentiment, however, when he sees his blinded father: "O gods! Who is't can say 'I am the worst'? / I am worse than e'er I was." He continues, "And worse I may be yet. The worst is not / As long as we can say 'This is the worst.'" When Gloucester hears that a madman is there, his speech indicates that he almost recognizes his son: "In the last night's storm I such a fellow saw, / Which made me think a man a worm. My son / Came then into my mind, and yet my mind / Was then scarce friends with him. I have heard more since."

A bit later, Gloucester delivers a wonderfully rich speech: "Let the superfluous and lust-dieted man / That stands your ordinance [resists heaven's command], that will not see / Because he does not feel, feel your power quickly. / So distribution should undo excess, / And each man have enough. Dost thou know Dover?" This seems to reflect on Lear, both his emotional blindness and the social woes he has overlooked, as in his own realization, "I have ta'en too little care of this." Some scholars favor a reading of the play in which Dover is seen as a symbol for a more progressive, less class-bound society, and this speech of Gloucester's is a mainstay of their argument.

PAGE 73: Goneril's original line is "I have been worth the whistling," a somewhat confusing reference to a dog who is (or is not) worth calling home.

PAGE 75: "And the queen" is my own addition, as it seems odd to me that the text says La Far is in charge yet he never appears in the play.

Some of my favorite imagery that appears throughout Shakespeare's plays is that of the natural elements as representations of characters' mental or emotional states. The storm in this play, which crescendos with Lear's grief, is the quintessential example. Another nice one appears in this conversation between Kent and the gentleman: "You have seen / sunshine and rain at once; her smiles and tears / Were like, a better way." I omitted it in favor of the king/rebel image, which seemed more indicative of the approaching conflict.

PAGE 76: I left out a passage in which the doctor goes on to say, essentially, that rest will cure Lear. This comes up a few times in the play, possibly suggesting that Shakespeare's view of health may have been that rest restores order and that no medical meddling is needed.

PAGE 77: I cut a line of Regan's, which I think unnecessary, though it does clarify why she wants Gloucester dead: "It was great ignorance, Gloucester's eyes being out, / To let him live. Where he arrives he moves / All hearts against us. Edmund, I think, is gone . . . to descry / The strength o' th' army."

PAGE 79: I changed *bourn* to *cliff* for clarity, and removed a passage in which Edgar invents an elaborate fantasy of seeing a demon on the top of the cliff, implying that malignant supernatural powers tried to aid Gloucester's suicide but good powers thwarted the attempt.

PAGE 80: In Lear's speech I changed *cause* to *crime* and *luxury* to *lechery,* for clarity. His rant goes on much longer, and includes a venomous attack on female sexuality, which I preferred to leave out, especially since the rest of the speech is more entertaining and (madly) astute.

PAGE 81: There's more great eye/sight imagery in this exchange between Lear and Gloucester:
L: "Read."
G: "What—with the case of eyes?"
L: "O ho, are you there with me? No eyes in your head, nor no money in your purse? Your eyes are in a heavy case, your purse in a light; yet you see how this world goes."
G: "I see it feelingly."

PAGE 83: I cut Edgar's description of himself as a poor man ready to lend a hand, which juxtaposes interestingly with Oswald's very different "friendly hand" on the next page.

PAGE 87: I took out "And the exchange my brother!" since the text of the letter makes this clear, and removing it streamlined the transition to the next line.

PAGE 88: I removed an exchange between Cordelia and Kent in which Cordelia asks Kent to remove his disguise and reconcile with Lear. Kent puts her off, saying, "Yet to be known shortens my made intent," meaning that he still has plans and reasons for wanting to stay incognito. Although it's implied that Kent is contriving in the background throughout the play, in the end his mysterious plots all fail to materialize. He has virtually no effect on the final outcome. Kent's failure is ultimately an important piece of the tragedy, but I don't find it thematically satisfying, as Shakespeare provides no explanation for it. I decided to show that Kent was wounded in the big battle, which crippled his ability to carry out his plans and protect his master. This fits a facet of Kent's personality established early in the play—that he relies too much on his physical capabilities.

PAGE 91: I cut "He's full of abdication and self-reproving," which parallels nicely with Lear as we've just seen him, similarly abdicated and self-reproving.

PAGE 92: *Touches* = concerns. The crux of Albany's speech is that he has decided to join his forces with Regan's because the French army is invading. His speech, though, indicates that his sympathy would be with Lear, if Lear were not allied with Cordelia and the French. Regan wants to take him to task for this, but Goneril forestalls their argument (presumably because she knows Albany's cooperation is quite delicate at this point, and she has lost her control over him). Albany's full speech to Regan reads: "Our very loving sister, well bemet, / For this I hear: the King is come to his daughter, / With others whom the rigour of our state/ Forced to cry out. Where I could not be honest / I never yet was valiant. For this business, / It touches us as France invades our land, / Yet bold's the King, with others whom, I fear. / Most just and heavy causes make oppose."

PAGE 97: Lear goes on at some length about what a nice time he and Cordelia can have in prison. He's clearly reconciled with his daughter, but perhaps not with reality: " . . . and laugh / At gilded butterflies, and hear poor rogues / Talk of court news, and we'll talk with them too— / Who loses and who wins, who's in, who's out, / And take upon 's the mystery of things / As if we were God's spies; and we'll wear out / In a walled prison packs and sects of great ones / That ebb and flow by th' moon."

PAGE 98: I used the shorter Folio line here for the captain's answer, but the Quarto reads, "I cannot draw a cart, / Nor eat dried oats. If it be man's work, I'll do 't," which I think is great characterization.

PANEL 4: Albany doesn't have a line here, but I made him start to issue an order so I could suggest that his intention is to settle matters with Lear right away, and that Edmund has to stall him.

PAGE 100: Edmund's "Let the drum strike and prove my title good" (to which I added "then" for rhythm) is instead said by Regan in the Folio—"Let the drum strike and prove my title thine"—but I prefer the Quarto version, suggesting that Edmund feels he already has the power of Regan's army. Albany is, of course, about to disabuse him of this notion, and this is really Albany's moment of triumph. As I see it, Albany, having been forewarned by Edgar, is leaving nothing to chance; so I have him bringing in his army to make sure Edmund is trapped. Visually in this scene I'm paying homage to *Ran,* the spectacular film by Akira Kurosawa which is based on *King Lear.* In Kurosawa's version of the big battle scene, the armies move rapidly around the field in centipede-like rivers of armored men, to great visual effect.

PAGE 109: In the original text, Edmund ends his "Who art thou" speech with "If thou 'rt noble, I do forgive thee." This is rather ironic, since his own nobility is the product of lies and treason.

Edgar's comment about "The dark and vicious place where thee he [be]got" suggests contempt for his father's sexual relations with women. Lear also seems to have little respect for women (see page 114 note), and the majority of female characters in this play are pretty rotten. By the end, all of them are dead. To see Shakespeare treat women in a more positive light, you might want to read *Twelfth Night* and *The Merchant of Venice.*

PAGE 110: Edgar also recounts meeting Kent after the battle, but doesn't provide any more clues as to exactly what Kent's plans were or how they failed.

PAGE 114: I cut out the sexist part of Lear's lament here. The full line is "Her voice was ever soft, Gentle, and low, an excellent thing in women." (Sigh.)

PAGE 115: In the original text, Kent explains that he was disguised as Lear's servant Caius. Since this is the only time a name is mentioned for Kent's alter ego, and since Lear doesn't seem to really comprehend what Kent is saying, I chose to omit this exchange. Some theatrical productions, however, do make this an emotional moment of reunion.

—*G. H.*

Copyright © 2007 by Gareth Hinds

First Candlewick Press editions 2009

Library of Congress Cataloging-in-Publication Data is available.
Library of Congress Catalog Card Number 2008938399
ISBN 978-0-7636-4343-0 (hardcover)
ISBN 978-0-7636-4344-7 (paperback)

2 4 6 8 10 9 7 5 3 1

Printed in China

This book was typeset in Weiss.
The illustrations were done in ink and watercolor,
with digital support.

Candlewick Press
99 Dover Street
Somerville, Massachusetts 02144

visit us at www.candlewick.com